READERS
REVEALED

D. S. LARANCE

DocUmeant *Publishing*
244 5th Avenue
Suite G-200
NY, NY 10001
646-233-4366
www.DocUmeantPublishing.com

Published by
DocUmeant Publishing
244 5th Ave, Suite G-200
NY, NY 10001
646–233-4366

This is a work of fiction. Names, characters, businesses, places, events and incidents are either the products of the author's imagination or used in a fictitious manner. Any resemblance to actual persons, living or dead, or actual events is purely coincidental.

Permission should be addressed in writing to the publisher at publisher@ DocUmeantPublishing.com

Editing by Philip S. Marks

Cover by Ginger Marks

Formatted by DocUmeant Designs, www.DocUmeantDesigns.com

Library of Congress Control Number: 2025931769
ISBN: 9781957832456 (pbk)
ISBN: 9781957832463 (epub)

This book is dedicated to my grandparents Ralph and Mildred Goldstrom who graciously adopted me as their own.

CONTENTS

Acknowledgments

Many thanks to my husband Tim who helped in the research, our daughter-in-law Stephanie proofing and advising, and all the many people who have inspired me to keep writing

PROLOGUE

CLAIRE BURKE SAT alone in her study, dozing as she read the pages of an article she had written years before. She remembered the words on the page, but whether they were real or fiction was unclear. In the far corner of the dimly lit room, she sat in an overstuffed chair with her feet tucked beneath her. This was her favorite room in the house. It was Nathan's room and it reminded her of England. How could she not love it? The furniture was rich Edwardian Mahogany, and the walls were papered in grass cloth. A huge bookcase that was full of books stood behind an enormous desk, each book positioned meticulously in its place. Nathan liked it that way.

Claire was especially drawn to the mahogany desk, which shone with fresh polish. There were only a few items on the desktop, but they were organized to best serve the person who would sit there. A strong, driven person . . . her Nathan. Oh how she wished he were here now. She always felt safe when Nathan was nearby.

Her musing was interrupted by a clanging from downstairs, followed by what she thought was a voice. Claire strained as she listened intently, but heard nothing more. She knew she would feel uneasy until Nathan returned and chastised herself for being such a fraidy-cat. Strengthening her resolve, she rustled up her nerve and called out in a timid voice, "Hello? Is someone there?"

No answer. She hated these nights when Nathan was out so late. Suddenly, a deafening crash of thunder caused her to shudder with fright at the onerous sounds of the storm. She wondered if a window shade had come loose and was banging around in the wind. Claire laughed at herself and thought of how much she had enjoyed scary movies when she was young. As the storm subsided, she could still hear the rain as it gently pattered on the porch's tin roof. At the soft echo of the rain, Claire began to relax. As if on cue, it occurred to her that a cup of tea would be just the thing. She put on her fuzzy pink slippers, pulled her bathrobe closer around her, and descended the beautiful wooden staircase that wound in a spiral to the first floor.

Since Claire was at the back of the house, the kitchen was just below her. She vowed not to have so much glass in her next home because she didn't like the way people could see in at night. Gingerly, she reached over and touched the light switch on the kitchen wall and then turned the circular knob to lower the lights to a warm glow.

The automatic kettle whistled as the water came to a boil before she could even get a cup and tea bag from the cabinet in front of her. Her ancestors would have been disappointed in her, as she preferred tea bags to the loose leaf tea steeped in the silver ball. It was so much easier to use a tea bag, and the taste was really about the same. After adding one lump of sugar she exited the kitchen, climbed the staircase, and entered the study.

Settling into her chair, glancing over at the clock, she was surprised to see that it was 1:45 a.m. Nathan was *very* late. His meetings normally didn't go past 10 p.m. Even when he went for a drink after, he was always home before midnight. Claire's thoughts turned back to the days when they had spent most of their time together. But Nathan had taken the promotion of a lifetime, and they moved away from everything she'd known her whole life. Deep in thought, she pulled her blanket up over her shoulders and sat deeper into the chair intending to fall asleep. She never liked going to bed without Nathan.

As Claire began to relax, her eyes fell on the painting hanging in the center of the wall. It was an old oil painting of a quaint village by an English artist. Nathan had purchased it for her just before they moved to the United States 25 years ago. It was a sort of peace offering that he had given her when he told her he had accepted the job in Washington, D.C. Her eyes were drawn to it now. Taking a deep breath she allowed herself to be pulled into the painting.

The quaint cobblestone street seemed to beckon her to come further into the center of town. It had been a brisk, glorious day, full of sunshine, with a hint of a cool breeze. She shivered as she recalled wishing she had brought her sweater.

The birds chirped vociferously, and she knew it was early spring. She looked at the budding trees all around the village. In another week or so, those buds would sprout and some of the sunshine would recede into the shadows. *Why did that give her pause?*

Claire glanced toward the infamous Afternoon Tearoom and realized she was a bit hungry. Her mouth watered as she thought of their grilled cheese sandwiches, the tearoom specialty, and she began to quicken her steps. It seemed like her legs 'wouldn't move any faster, and she became disoriented. She paused a moment to catch her breath. *What is wrong with me?* She could see the tearoom up ahead behind a large group of pine trees. Just as she started out again, she thought she heard someone calling her name. "Nathan?" she whispered and looked back but saw no one. Oddly, somehow she was now standing at the door to the tearoom. It was very heavy, and she struggled to get it open. *Why did she feel so weak?* To her surprise the tearoom was very noisy, although there didn't seem to be very many people inside. It was extremely dark so, she hesitated just inside the door to let her eyes adjust to the dimness of the room.

"Claire, over here!" *Was that Nina's voice? How could Nina be here?* As she peered into the darkness she saw someone waving wildly at her. The thought of seeing her childhood friend again brought tears to her eyes. She tried to move her feet and stumbled down the few stairs just inside the doorway. Once she regained her footing, she looked up and saw Nina walking toward her. Claire tried to walk toward her, but her knees gave way and she fell into a chair placed just off to the side of the stairs, certain if she didn't sit down, she would fall. Nina walked right past her without even looking at her. Her eyes followed Nina toward the doorway and realized the din in the room had become inaudible. She looked around and noticed everyone was looking at a cloaked man who stood just inside the doorway. He was dripping wet.

Nina hugged the man, oblivious of him being wet, and the two of them turned back toward Claire. Their faces were still in the shadows but she could see they were exchanging softly spoken words, as if they had a secret. Their faces slowly came into view and Claire recognized her husband's face and captivating smile. "Nathan," she whispered. Excited at that moment, she felt happy to see him.

"What are you doing here?" she asked as she reached up to him. Nathan stooped in front of her and picked her up in his arms. Holding her firmly to his chest, he began to swing her around playfully.

"Where am I dear Claire?" He said mysteriously and began to laugh. Claire laughed too as he swung her off her feet and held her in his arms. She was spinning; the room was going around faster and faster. Suddenly, she felt a blanket fly around her and cover her face. As she began to struggle, she begged Nathan to put her down. In the background she could hear Nina's laughter, and the din was back. It too was filled with laughter. She tried to grab the blanket and began to thrash around wildly.

"Stop it! Nathan, Please Stop it!" she heard her own voice pleading.

And then, it stopped.

"In the echoes of solitude, even the shadows of memory can be hauntingly comforting."

~ Debbie Larance

CHAPTER ONE

THE SKY WAS gray with clouds, whispered of the rain to come. Somehow, it seems appropriate for this day. The long funeral procession enters the quiet cemetery through a back entrance, as if it has something to hide. Their life together is over, their goals unfulfilled. Nathan stands staring at the cold, stone grave marker barely controlling his anger. The words, "Beloved Wife," were carved into its granite surface. His hands at his sides flexed into fists, and he forced them to relax. Anger wasn't quite the right word; it was darker than anger. This was an affront to him, personally. No, this was not over at all. Now, it was his fight.

Nina Cavanaugh, Claire's best friend, stands beside him holding his elbow. She is wearing a fitted purple suit, matching hat, heels, and clutch. Her funeral attire was designed to show off her slim figure, something Claire had always admired about Nina. Her curly red hair was pulled up under a hat with a short purple veil hiding her eyes. Nina's ensemble, which she had spent quite a long time picking out, was stunning and had cost her a week's salary.

As she remains stoically beside Nathan, her mind drifts back to the past. She was sorry she hadn't made a better effort to stay in contact once Claire and Nathan moved to the US. Nina regretted that she hadn't come to the states to visit them even though Claire had invited her several times. She couldn't help but think Washington was a surprisingly beautiful city, now that she was here. She had always thought the old world power of London was superior to anything in the New World. But as she looked around, she saw monuments, stately buildings, well laid out and full of powerful people. Nina admired nothing more than real power.

Truth be told, she was sorry she had ever introduced Claire to Nathan and wondered if Claire might still have been alive if she hadn't. Nina shook her head thinking there was no point lamenting over past mistakes. Watching the cold rain falling, she noticed people begin to cover their heads and retreat to their limos. *Even Mother Nature cried for Saint Claire, how appropriate,* Nina mused silently.

There was a small tent over the gravesite, but the rain kept blowing harder, and water was beginning to stream downhill toward the open grave. The cemetery crew stood at a short distance, anxiously waiting to lower the casket into its final resting place before the grave became compromised. Nathan noticed Nina patting her eyes and reached into his coat pocket and handed her his handkerchief. Acting the fair maiden, she sniffed a little harder attempting a demure posture that she didn't really feel. *This nasty rain is about to ruin my makeup.* Nathan took her elbow and encouraged her to walk with him toward their limo. Always the gentleman, he held his coat over her head to shield her from the cold rain which threatened to soak them both.

Once they were in the limo, Nathan whispered, "How appropriate for it to rain." The smile on his face strangely distant in his eyes, "Claire loved to sit outside under the porch's tin roof and listen to the rain." He mused at the pleasant memory. "As a matter of fact it was raining the night she died." Nina kept silent, not particularly remembering any affinity Claire might have had to rain.

The ride back to the house was eerily silent as they both became lost in their own thoughts.

Nathan had spared no expense when he arranged for cooks and servers to handle the formalities of Claire's wake. His home, although always beautiful, had been transformed into a perfect tribute to his beloved wife. There were flowers from all over the world sent by friends and various dignitaries placed here and there around the house. Several special photos of Nathan and Claire had been cleaned up and set out for people to admire. There was a bartender and an extensive liquor cabinet that would be wide open today. And of course, the cooks had spent hours creating special canapés, and hors d'oeuvres to tempt and treat the wide variety of guests that would enjoy his hospitality in honor of his wife. If nothing else, Nathan expected to give the impression of affluence and privilege throughout his home. He wanted his friends and co-workers to get the impression Claire was the perfect wife and he the luckiest man around, until today.

Nina was genuinely impressed with the house, the grounds, and the furnishings. The house was gorgeous with a circular driveway and the big white columns that graced the entryway. She thought back to the day Claire told Nina of her dream that one day her home would have a big circular driveway. Nina smiled at the thought of how they both had giggled at her outrageous dream.

"Well, you made it kiddo!" she whispered to herself. And of course, Claire had been right, there was plenty of room for Nina to come for a visit and stay a while. Claire had always liked the look of rich wood tones, "real furniture" she called it, and she had spared no expense making her dream home a reality. Nina found it a little difficult to remember her friend Claire versus this Claire. She didn't really know *this* Claire.

Nina sat watching the people mill around with no idea who she was watching. She recognized the uniforms of apparently important people and could tell some of the guests had personal bodyguards with them. Several others needed interpreters. She'd known, of course, that Nathan held an important position with the U.S. Intelligence Service, but neither he nor Claire ever spoke of the details.

In turn, the guests were all very curious about this friend of Claire's who had come so far, so quickly, to stay with Nathan ... only after Claire had passed away. Where had she been when her best friend had been so ill? Several of the ladies took the time to speak to Nina in hopes of gathering details, but Nina was quite adept at teasing them with very little legitimate information. Nina had no doubt several of the ladies were eyeing Nathan as a prospect for a daughter or niece as he was obviously in need of a new wife, after a decent amount of mourning time, of course.

Normally a good host, today, Nathan sat quietly in his chair nursing one drink after another. The chair next to him, Claire's chair, had been occupied by any number and variety of people expressing their sympathies. Nina remained next to him for quite some time but could not keep track of them all. She noticed that when she was around, conversations tapered off to whispers, indicating the guests were unwilling to talk freely around her. She did not understand that in the military world, especially the spy world, it was an unspoken custom not to chat openly around those you do not know. It was not meant to be a slight against Nina personally, although it was making her feel very much an outsider. She couldn't help wondering if this was how Claire had felt.

As the sun went down most of the guests had departed. The room was growing quite dark when the Sergeant at Arms of the Honor Guard assigned to Nathan today, approached her. The young man, who may have been all of 21 years old, let her know that as soon as the kitchen crew had departed for the evening, they would also be leaving. Nina didn't really understand that part of their function for the day was to make certain Nathan was "taken care of" until the function was over. Someone at Nathan's level in the CIA who had access to extensive top-secret information needed to be protected when they were most vulnerable, as Nathan was today. They watched whom he spoke to and who spoke to him not let him out of their sight for a moment.

Having no way of knowing what she was expected to do, she simply smiled sitting down next to Nathan who now rested in his comfortable chair, fast asleep.

When she was the only person in the house left awake, Nina headed upstairs. She hated to leave Nathan asleep in the chair, but truth be told, the enormous house gave her the creeps. Nina headed directly for the study which she knew was Claire's favorite place to sit. As she stepped inside, she paused wrapping her arms around herself as a chill ran through her. Glancing around the room, she half expecting to see Claire watching her. Turning back around, she noticed an array of papers on the desk and wondered if Nathan had been looking for something specific. Logic told her that perhaps the police had rummaged around in the desk when they came in response to Nathan's call.

A large, stately, rich mahogany desk and with a chair behind it called to her, so Nina rounded the desk sitting down in it.

For several minutes she found herself enjoying a quiet respite. Eventually, her focus was drawn to the blank space on the wall in front of the desk where Claire's favorite painting should be hanging. Nina had never seen "the painting", but she had heard plenty about it. Nina felt certain she knew what haunted Claire, and just thinking about it brought old feelings back to life. It saddened her knowing how tormented Claire had been by it all. Nina had been anxious to see the painting. *What has Nathan done with it?* She shook free of the old memories and began to look for the one story that might have the answers. Opening the drawers and thumbing through its contents, she spied what she was looking for in the bottom drawer of the desk, in an old stationery box with the word Applebee engraved on the top.

Carefully, she opened the knotted string tied around the box and looked inside. An old photograph of her sitting in Nathan's old Austin was taped to the top page. She smiled as she remembered that day. This was the first trip she and Claire had taken to Applebee. She wished with all her heart she could go back in time and change that day. She began reading and in the next minute felt another chill, this one like no other. *What would Nathan think of her if he found out?*

> Most people don't believe in witchcraft. I never did. But sometimes when you are unable to explain mysterious events, witchcraft is as good an explanation as any. I suppose often there are other explanations, and what happens when those are more unbelievable than witchcraft. You must consider whether or not you know all the facts, and whether or not your sources are accurate. But sometimes, your reality is challenged beyond what you expect. I want to tell you a story of a little village outside London. It starts on a beautiful spring morning. . . .
>
> My friend Nina and I drove to the country in Nathan's old, run-down car in search of the truth about a nursery rhyme. I'd always heard most nursery rhymes

have some twisted truth behind their story, so in a way I was prepared for anything.

When I met Nina, we both lived at an orphanage just outside of London, and we attended an all-girls' school with some of the neighboring children from town. The school, known simply as The London School for Girls, was old. It was run by a foundation that had meager resources, which meant frills were non-existent and necessities were old and tattered. A nearby church sent several nuns each day to help with tutoring and, to everyone's relief, some lunch at midday.

Nina's family had abandoned her after the death of her mother. We often fantasized that her family must be very rich and thus eccentric so we expected that any day they would return for her, having realized their great mistake.

I knew my parents had been killed in an accident while skiing in some foreign country, and none of my known relatives were willing to take me in. We used to enjoy telling people we were sisters, but nobody ever believed us, as Nina was very tall with dark red overly curly hair and freckles. She was very feminine, sneaky, and a little squeamish. I was much shorter, very blonde, and a tomboy through and through. Why we got along was anyone's guess, but we both enjoyed writing stories and making up tales that almost certainly ended with us being found out to be sisters from a family of unlimited resources.

One day, as part of a class, our teacher told us a story about a local village mired in a mysterious few lines of poetry. The assignment was to memorize the poem and recite it in front of the class using different speech patterns. Nina and I made up an entire story behind the poem where a group of Scottish hooligans that were running from the law had settled in the little village. We practiced the rhyme with the Scottish brogue so much that we both got an A on the assignment.

Applebee town is a beautiful place with fresh waters running nearby too,

The village is old and stands in disrepair, lo' the shame wash over you.

If it's not your home, the time you spend there will come at a heavy cost,

The town takes its toll, as it's taking your soul, you will wander and ever be lost.

Neither Nina nor I ever thought of going to Applebee until I took a job as a writer at Britain's favorite tabloid. At first, I was satisfied to write articles about recipes, or fashion, and of course the royal family. Eventually, I got restless and needed a challenge. Maybe a story with some real meat to it. But it was 1964 and nobody cared what a woman thought when it came to the real news, especially during war time.

One afternoon, after I'd put my two assigned columns to bed, I sat with my editor, Mr. Wiltshire, having a cup of tea. He was a stern older man who had worked at the paper most of his life and hadn't actually decided if women working was a good idea (after a while he softened and acted more like a grandpa). This day, I came right out and asked if he would trust me with a more interesting article. After he yammered for a few minutes, which was one of his habits to allow himself time to think, his face lit up as if he'd just had a brilliant notion. He asked if I'd ever heard of the Applebee rhyme? I told him that of course I had heard of the rhyme, but that I felt certain it was just clever lines of prose written by some fanciful old man for publicity. Mr. Wiltshire assured me he had very good reason to believe the story was not just fancy? When he saw I was hesitant he called me on my honor, "If you don't think you can handle it . . ." I flashed him my most brilliant smile, fully aware of how I was being played, and took the paper he was handing me, "Oh, I can handle it, alright, but I'll bet you a shilling it turns out to be some sort of scandal within the ranks of the town?" I didn't say so to Mr. Wiltshire, but it was definitely more interesting than writing about recipes.

I was proud of myself. I had gone after what I wanted in the business world and won. It is not a common thing these days, even though there is talk of women taking over the world. Everyone knows that is a huge exaggeration. Now, I have to see if I could do the same at home. I needed to borrow Nathan's car and didn't want to tell him why. I wasn't sure how he would feel about me being an investigative journalist. At worst, he would want to come along and, in a creepy way, that reminded me more of a father than of a husband. Along with a little light pouting, I told Nathan that Nina and I were going shopping and had heard there were some excellent shops in a little village just outside London and I knew he would not want me on the train without him. His expression, as I spoke, told me I had guessed correctly. A day of shopping with two women was not something Nathan would enjoy, and he actually 'suggested' we take the car. I was genuinely surprised and happy I did not have to lie, well not totally, to my wonderful husband. Now, I just had to talk Nina into coming "shopping" with me.

I put off talking to Nina until the day before I was to go. I knew I could trust Nina, my best friend, not to laugh at me or tell Nathan of my deceit. I was correct. Being orphans, neither of us had much experience traveling outside the city or driving cars. This was indeed going to be an adventure for both of us.

Nina showed up at my apartment right after Nathan left for work. She was dressed in a light blue sundress with a jacket. Her matching shoes were quite old, and her purse was the same one she had carried for the last two years. The flowered scarf accented her outfit perfectly and succeeded in making me look frumpy.

I was wearing my usual style of blue jeans and pink sweater. I had always been called the pretty one, with my long blond hair and girly figure, but Nina ran circles around me in style. I dressed for comfort and Nina was all about fashion.

It was an uneventful drive and didn't take as long as we expected. We went directly to Applebee and upon arriving ran into our first snag. Accessing Applebee by car was difficult at best. It took us awhile to realize that they had created a small parking area outside the town, and expected folks to walk in.

It was a darling little town and reminded me of a picturesque post card. The downtown streets were mostly cobblestone and very narrow. They would not work well with a car. Not only were they not big enough, but the cobblestone would probably be destroyed with much traffic driving on it. The parking situation probably limited the visitation during the snowy time of year, but otherwise, in my opinion, it added a charming ambiance.

The buildings were very old, made of stone with the traditional peaks and towers of the period. As we walked around, we found the village was larger than it appeared from the road, and the homes were well-hidden—until you got deeper into town. When you had almost crossed through town, you came to a surprisingly large river that seemed to flow swiftly. We sat on the riverbank for a long while we enjoyed the cool breeze. Eventually, we realized our need to find a place to get lunch, as we had both skipped breakfast in our hurry to get started on our adventure.

We chose a place called the Afternoon Tearoom, which was a Tudor style building that looked dismal and run down. The huge front door opened into a small dark foyer with two staircases running off of it. A few steps down led to a large dining area with a bar and long wooden tables, much like what you might expect in an alehouse from years ago. We did not investigate where the other stairs went, but assumed there were rooms to let up there. To our relief, inside the establishment was quite well maintained.

The waitresses were dressed in frilly white peasant tops with blue jeans, quite appropriate for the ambience of the place. We were handed menus and welcomed by a short red-haired young lady. The blush on her cheeks looked natural and made us wonder if she was too warm. We noticed there was a large fire in the fireplace across the room on the outside wall. It was a beautiful day, but if you were just sitting about in an old damp building, you might get a chill. There were not many patrons in the place and soon another waitress came to take our orders. She was quite lovely and, to our good fortune, very friendly. When we expressed curiosity about the village, she was more than willing to tell us everything she knew about the place although most of it was village gossip and not history.

The waitress recommended the grilled cheese sandwich or the beef stew, which we learned had been made just this morning. We gave her our lunch order and prodded her to continue chatting by asking if she knew about the poem. Her expression told us she had never heard of it.

When she returned with a cup of soup for each of us, she told us that Frank Smythe, the Duke of Applebee's son was standing at the bar. He would be able to help us; of course, we were excited to meet him.

The waitress went over to a rather large man, dressed in gentlemanly attire, interrupted his conversation with another less splendidly attired gentleman, and *pointed over at us. He dismissed his companion and headed toward our booth.*

The conversation was very polite, and we each played our parts outstandingly. We tried to get him to offer to show us around, but he was unable to do so. He did tell us that the grounds had been given to his great grandfather, Lawton Smythe, in 1814. King George, III himself had gifted it to them for services rendered, but he didn't say what the services were. At that time, it was called Harleysville. His grandfather changed the name to Applebee in deference to his wife, Mildred Applebee.

We asked a few more questions about the area, the name of the river going by Applebee Junction and were also told it was dug only to serve Applebee and that it joins the Thames about a mile from town. It was dredged to assist with shipping.

Our sandwiches came and we asked Frank to join us, but he declined and indicated his lunch hour was over and that he needed to get back to work. He seemed like a fine gentleman. I did think it unusual that an educated man knew so little about his hometown's history, when it had been his family's home since 1851. I would expect family pride, especially that of a Duke, would be reason enough to know more. I can't help but wonder if he was hiding something.

Nina and I chatted the entire way back to London. I dropped her off at her flat, and suggested we go back sometime soon. I think she may have been more excited about that notion than I was myself.

—

Nina glanced up at the old grandfather clock in the hall and realized it was past midnight. She could barely keep her eyes open, and knew she needed to go to bed. She found herself sitting in the desk chair full of old memories . She was bursting with emotions that she knew would not let her rest. Thinking back to those old days hurt in so many ways. Now that Claire was dead, she knew she was going to have to deal with them alone.

Remembering the story Claire had printed in the paper about Applebee Nina knew it had been watered down. Mr. Wiltshire had never asked her to write another feature. At the time Nina thought it was because the Applebee article was not very good. None of the adventure and excitement they had felt came across in the article. But maybe these pages had captured the story of two young innocents, and their first adventure as grown-ups during a turbulent time. Claire's personality was evident in these few pages. Nina tried not to think of where all this had led to, but the memories loomed in front of her like an angry ghost. Carefully, she laid the papers back in the box for another day, retying the string so it didn't look like it had been disturbed. As she slipped it back into the desk drawer, she wondered why she'd done that.

When Nina woke the next morning, her mind was full of the good old days. It was as if she was reliving them. Claire was right there with her, reminding her of why they were best friends. She had been a smart and funny little girl, full of life and curiosity. Most would agree Claire was a tomboy. She loved to be outdoors, running, climbing the biggest trees, and she swam like a fish. Nina had always been more interested in not messing up her clothes. She envied the way Claire could play with abandon.

More than anything Nina remembered how kind Claire had always been. She cared about everything! A vision of a little bird that had fallen out of its nest in the big oak tree next to their bedroom window at the orphanage flashed into her mind. Claire had climbed up that big old tree and put the little creature back in the nest, only to have the momma bird kick it out again. Claire kept the little bird in a box and fed it squished up worms to try and nurse it back to health. Then she cried half the night when the frail little thing died anyway.

Nina recalled how Claire had been awarded a full scholarship to a little city college. She insisted Nina work hard and come with her. Nina knew she would never have bothered if it hadn't been for Claire. They had lived over the stable at a nearby ranch where Claire helped care for the horses to help pay their rent. In Nina's mind it was way too much nasty work for very little reward. But Claire did it happily and would have done it for free just to be near the horses. Nina on the other hand was paid to clean the owner's house on Saturday for her part of the rent.

After graduation, they stayed together in a small two-bedroom apartment in London. Nina remembered how happy she had been to eliminate the stable smell from her daily life. The diminutive apartment was on the third floor, but it had two bedrooms, so it was the first time the girls had any privacy for themselves. They had made out a chore list and agreed to make time every Friday night to do something together, even if it was just to go out to dinner. It seemed a small thing, but with their respective work schedules, some days they wouldn't even see each other at all.

Nina had worked at a bank as a teller, it was a decent job, and she was glad to have it. She dreamed of being a pediatrician and knew she had years of school ahead of her. It wasn't easy, but she was determined. Claire had two part-time jobs, and also continued to go to school pursuing a degree in communications and journalism. Writing was her passion; she just wasn't sure what kind of writing suited her best, but Claire always enjoyed stretching herself to the limit. She worked at a bookstore four days out of the week, and then she worked as a freelance reporter at a small weekend newspaper. She didn't have actual hours at the paper. She would write articles she thought would be of interest and if they used them, she would get paid. She also helped with the society page articles when there was a need. Two single ladies living the good life, in a tattered apartment, with worn out furnishings and tattered clothes. They were young, healthy, and looking forward to something better.

One other memory pervaded Nina's mind. She tried not to think of it, but there was a part of her that cherished the tale. This morning she allowed herself to be drawn into the memory. Leaning into her pillow and picking up a second pillow that lay beside her and began hugging it as if it could somehow hug her back. She smiled as she saw herself actually meeting Nathan before Claire did. They usually attended the USO dances together after Friday night dinner. But that night Claire had to work late at the bookstore, and Nina had gone ahead by herself. She took a table by the dance floor, and almost heard herself giggle when she saw Nathan walking toward her. He was about as perfect as a male specimen could be. Tall, with broad shoulders, he sauntered as he walked toward her as if she was his prey. She'd always wondered if she could get male attention without Claire around. She could still hear him say, "Would you like to dance?" and noted the American accent that sounded almost barbaric. He took her hand and lifted her from her chair and into his arms leaving her no opportunity to say no. One dance had led to two, then three, until she'd lost count.

Eventually, he led her back to her table and whispered he'd be back with drinks. He returned quickly with wine, and they sat and talked for what seemed like forever. "Would you like to go get some dinner; I know this great little Italian place?"

She had eaten, but she said yes anyway. Smiling to herself, she ignored it when his friends hooted and whistled at Nathan as they walked toward the door. Nina remembered being relieved that they had left before Claire arrived.

Nathan took her to a candle lit bistro for dinner. In hindsight, it had been a night of seduction from the moment he took her in his arms. As they sat sipping their dessert wine, she was actually surprised to hear herself invite Nathan back to her place, the same place she shared with Claire. They hadn't even heard Claire come in that night. Nathan hadn't been her first, but she knew now he was her forever.

Nina shook herself out of her enchanted memory realizing she was close to searching Nathan out and seducing him if she continued. She got up and threw on her new bathrobe specifically chosen to display her charms and went downstairs.

Nathan was sitting at the table pretending to read the newspaper. His breakfast had been eaten, and his cup of coffee was steaming, apparently too hot to drink. Looking up at her he immediately saw through her obvious plan to attract him, "Nina, what are you doing?"

"Drinking a cup of coffee." Her British accent showing indignation as she realized she was about to be rejected. *Nathan saw through me all too quickly.* Trying to retain her composure she sat at the table across from him with her own cup of coffee. Apparently, all politeness was over as her stomach rumbled.

"First, I'd appreciate it if you would get dressed before coming downstairs. You never know who else might be around, and I'd rather not have to field questions about there being anything between us." Nathan paused realizing his gruffness sounded much harsher than he had intended.

Being a very astute student of human nature Nina retreated, "I'm sorry Nathan. I certainly did not mean to infer our relationship was anything, other than what it is." Nina apologized but allowed the sash on her robe to fall loose revealing her shoulder and part of a breast "Can't control yourself old boy?" she sassed.

"I didn't mean to be so severe, Nina." Nathan sipped his coffee, apparently oblivious to Nina's distraction. He decided a complete change of topic was required, "I noticed you were in the study last night, were you looking for something in particular?"

"Just things that remind me of Claire." she said innocently, tying her robe tightly around her. "What did you do with the painting?"

"I've had it packed. I hate that damn thing."

Nina studied Nathan a short while, "Will you tell me what happened to her, Nathan?"

"I've told you most of it already." He paused for a long sip of his coffee, then realizing there was nothing for her to eat he added, "I'm sorry Nina, are you hungry?"

"A little, but I can wait until lunch." She wondered if he was trying to avoid the subject and didn't want anything to interrupt their conversation. "I know you told me some, but I want to hear everything." Nina realized she sounded indelicate and hoped Nathan hadn't noticed.

"That's absurd Nina, I can't remember everything!" he shot back. Noticing the slight tinge of excitement in her curiosity he thought it totally out of line. He continued in a more contemplative manner, "She just seemed to slip away, she slowly became forgetful. She was always my sweet loving Claire, that never changed. But it was like a piece of her was just . . . gone."

Nina quietly observed him as he spoke. His remarkable love for Claire was still evident and she struggled not to show disappointment.

Nathan continued, "Then there was that painting. We attended an art auction one afternoon before we left London, and she fell absolutely in love with this painting by, I believe his name was Constable, an English painter. So of course, I bought it for her." Nathan seemed sullen as if he was sorry he'd bought it at all. "She became increasingly obsessed with it. She would just sit and stare at it for hours on end."

Wanting to know more, Nina and hoping she was being delicate enough not to upset Nathan any further she asked, "Did you take her for help? A therapist?"

"Of course I did. They did some tests, and after that she didn't want to go back. I thought maybe she was afraid they might find something." Nathan explained. "The doctors suspected some kind of brain damage," Nathan said as if it was the most absurd notion.

Reaching out Nina patted Nathan's hand. "Thank you, I understand better, it must have been horrible for you." She had decided not to poke at it any further, it sounded like dangerous territory for Nathan to relive.

But he continued, "It was hard to watch her just sort of fade away." Suddenly, he seemed to shake off the topic and blurted out, "I don't think it's a good idea for you to stay here, Nina."

"Why not?" Nina asked both surprised and a little offended. She liked it here and had hoped to make it a long holiday, before returning home.

"We need to be careful." He paused then as if he needed to explain himself, he continued, "Impressions you know. I have a reputation to think of."

"You think people will think we . . ." She almost felt a hypocrite when she herself was hoping . . .

"Well . . . of course . . . they already think it, but we can't give them a reason to suspect it." he answered briskly, cutting her off.

Nina wondered at his concern, but decided it was best not to fight it. "My return ticket is not for three more days."

"You can change it; you should leave tomorrow." Nathan never allowed for argument when he'd made up his mind.

"Tomorrow it is then." disappointment dripping in her voice. *If I am to leave tomorrow, I have a few things I wanted to get done before I leave.* She stood up and said, "You didn't answer me about the shopping trip Claire and I made. Did she ever tell you about it?"

"What shopping trip?"

"To this little village not far outside London."

"Oh, you mean back then, Applebee?" Nina was a little surprised, but nodded her head as he continued, in a much more upbeat manner. "She talked about it all the time. Some of the things she said . . . well, they sounded ridiculous."

"Oh dear!" Nina was surprised Claire had told Nathan about their adventures, and he didn't believe her. "Did she tell you it was an assignment from her editor?"

"Yeah, I actually called him and asked what he asked her to do."

"What did he say?" Nina asked with a little trepidation sneaking into her voice.

"He said it was to investigate a nursery rhyme." He shook his head in disbelief!

"We used to sing it as children"," Nina smiled fondly at the thought.

"I didn't understand how badly it bothered her," Nathan sagged as if from guilt.

"What exactly did she tell you?" Nina asked softly.

Nathan sighed heavily, "I don't remember, Nina I didn't really listen."

After a long drawn out pause Nina remarked, "I told you about it, Nathan. Remember, the beggar you met in London the night we went to dinner?" Nathan thought back to a trip he had taken to London about two years ago on business. He and Nina had gotten together for dinner to catch up and he took the opportunity to tell her a little of what Claire was going through at that time. Nina had shared some things with him that had surprised him and led him to some upsetting conclusions. While they were there, a street man came up and spoke to Nina for a time. She said he was begging for money. Without thinking about it, Nina confided to Nathan the man was a witch from Applebee. When Nathan questioned her, she told him there was nothing much to tell. But in reality, she knew she had said too much. At the time she knew that a man like Nathan was never oblivious to the details, and she wasn't sure what he might think or do should he put the pieces together.

Rummaging through Claire's things during the afternoon, Nathan and Nina were trying to see if there was anything important or interesting that they should discuss before she left. They uncovered some old photos and went through them carefully, noting who was identified on the back. Nathan gave Nina several of the pictures of people he did not know but kept a few that he found exceptionally interesting for one reason or another. The afternoon turned out to be very enjoyable, as they shared many wonderful memories while letting go of some of the sadder ones.

Realizing it was getting dark, they broke for dinner. Nathan originally thought he would take Nina out for a fancy dinner, but instead they decided on a local pizza joint that he and Claire enjoyed on many occasions. The proprietor, a stout gentleman named Tony, recognized Nathan and greeted him heartily expressing condolences over the loss of his wife. Nina was introduced as Claire's best friend from England and rewarded with a big hug and pat on the back after which they were led to a corner booth. Nathan told Nina to trust him and ordered the biggest, most delicious pizza Nina had ever eaten, and a pitcher of beer. Taking a sip of her beer, Nina remarked that she felt Americans were a bit too gregarious for her taste. Nathan's eyes twinkled with mirth as he explained how he and Claire had dined here frequently, and most Americans pride themselves on giving personal friendly service. He went on to explain that Tony knew he had just lost his wife, and wanted to understand who this woman was that Nathan brought into such a personal spot so soon after Claire's funeral. "Human Nature," Nathan stated.

Nodding her head at his explanation she said, "It truly is delicious, Nathan, with all the meats." Nina was truly delighted as she stuffed another slice of pizza into her mouth. She was beginning to wonder if Nathan had always been so American.

"Claire liked it too," Nathan smiled while reaching for another slice. The time flew and by the end of the evening they realized that they had been sitting in the booth for over three hours. No less than three people Nathan knew had come in and stopped by to say hello. One couple, Billie and Kyle Johnson, Nathan was particularly happy to see. Billie was the daughter of Richard, one of Nathan's old military buddies. The couple sat with them until their own pizza came out of the oven. As they left, Nathan told her that her father would remember Nina; to be sure to tell him she'd seen her. At that Billie took out her cell phone and asked Kyle to take a photo of the three of them, so she could show her dad.

"Dad is in New York now you know?" Billie informed Nathan.

"He is? On business?"

"Yes, he has an office, very legit now, you know." She smiled and gave her Uncle Nathan a big hug.

"It was a fun night, Nathan, but I still cannot remember Richard." Nina commented as they paid their bill.

"Yes, we deserved a little fun after the week we've had." Nathan responded, nodding at Tony, who nodded back knowingly, he intentionally ignored Nina's comment about Richard. He could not believe Nina had forgotten him so completely.

"I wish Claire could have joined us." Nina's expression did not tell of her true feelings. Nathan put his arms around her and patted her back. Actually, he had begun to wonder if Nina's feelings were genuine. Turning, Nathan waved at Tony as the door closed behind them.

"I'm going to put on a pot of coffee, if you'd like any." Nathan called as they entered the house.

"Maybe later, I need to get packed. My plane leaves at 2 o'clock."

"Let's plan to leave about eleven that way we can run by the cemetery on the way." Nathan headed to the kitchen and Nina climbed the stairs to her room.

She hadn't brought much with her, so it didn't take too long to get everything packed. When Nathan came up with a cup of coffee for each of them, he found her in the study, reading.

"Interesting story?"

"It's about our trips to Applebee," Nina explained.

Nathan nodded at her and said, "I'll leave you to it, then."

Thursdays seem to be the best day for me to go out investigating my assignment. Some of the locals are getting friendly with me, and call me by name, but I can never seem to remember theirs. They say I am asking all the same questions I asked before. My notes do not show these questions being asked, so I think they are playing tricks on me because they like their privacy.

I did some research at the public library today and have some specific questions I want answered. It turns out Applebee had a small historical society and a church that contains a community bible where births and deaths are traditionally recorded. I also found a rudimentary map of the village dating back about 100 years. The village has not really grown, but many things have been renamed. I wonder why?

Nina and I decided to walk through the entire downtown district. I realized they had horse posts around the downtown area with water troughs. Apparently, some people still ride horses into town, which is unusual these days. Nina and I stopped at the River Wharf for a sandwich and asked some questions of an old man behind the counter pouring beer. He was very friendly, and wanted to flirt with us but otherwise was disappointing. He said the historical society that also served as a small library had burned down 10 years ago and it was never replaced.

Frustration is getting the best of me. It never occurred to me that the information in the library could be that old. I asked what they do when they need to know what happened in the past. He told me they asked the Smythe family if they knew. I sarcastically asked him if the Smythe family owned the town, and he told me they did. Outright owned the town. Imagine that?

I had to get home early today because Nathan was worried last week when I wasn't there when he got home from work. I don't want him to worry about me, so I need to get supper on the table for him on time. ❦

It was a rainy day today, and I probably should not have driven all the way to the country by myself. But I was so excited to go to the church to hopefully get some real information about the village. I hope I will soon have enough to begin the article for the paper. Nina could not come today as she has a big test at her doctoral college.

I went to the church and was greeted by what I assume was the priest. I asked if they had the community Bible. He told me they did but it had been housed in a damp cellar for so long, the pages had gotten very wet, the ink on the pages had run, and it was virtually illegible. I asked him if I could see it anyway and identified myself as a reporter for the London Sun researching old records. Nothing specific, just how old records were stored. He seemed to be happy with that explanation and took me down two long flights of stone stairs to a very damp, very dark cellar. It was impossible to read the writing in such dark surroundings, so I asked if I could bring it up the stairs into the light. He asked me not to and instead lit a torch hanging in a cup nailed to the wall and held it down to light up the bible. Can you believe it? I suppose it doesn't matter anyway.

The priest asked if I was looking for someone specific in the book. I didn't answer and found my way back to the staircase to leave. I am very disappointed, as nothing I try seems to give me any information about the town. I realize that if anyone in the town would know if there had ever been witches in Applebee, it would be the priest. "Why not?" I asked him. The priest stopped and looked at me with a curious expression on his face but to my surprise he said not for many years. Stories indicate back in the 1700s there was a family of witches that called Harleysville home.

I told him about the poem, and he began to quote it to back me. He said it had been years since anyone came asking about it. I asked him if he knew where it originated and he told me a story of a jilted suitor who wrote the poem to scare away other prospective suitors. I thought that made as much sense as anything else had and asked the suitor's name. "Legible." I wrote the name down so I wouldn't forget it. I asked if he knew who Mr. Legible wrote the poem for and was told, "Mildred Applebee." At that, I turned and left the church and drove home quickly so I would arrive in time to have dinner on the table before Nathan came home. I mentioned the name Legible to Nina and she said she met someone with that same name in Applebee. She promised to introduce me to him on the next visit we make together.   ✄

———

Today I went back to the library to do some research on the names Legible and Smythe. I have been concerned that it has been so long, there wouldn't be much information still available. To my surprise, I found out the Legible family has lived in the area for a very long time and at one time even claimed to own much of the land in Applebee or Harleysville, as it was known then. There is even a Legible family still living in the village. Their ownership ended when King George gave the property to Lawton Smythe, who as we know, married Mildred Applebee and changed the name of the town.

Tomorrow I am going to ask Nina to come with me to rent a horse and ride toward the Smythe estate. I'll just poke around and get an idea of what it is like. Maybe, I'll even run into a couple of people who won't mind chatting about the Legible or Smythe families.   ✄

———

Realizing it had gotten quite late, Nina decided she would not be able to finish reading Claire's notes while she was still here. There were still too many pages yet to review. She decided to ask Nathan to make her a copy so she could continue reading Claire's journal back in London. Making her way to her bedroom she was soon fast asleep. Exhausted, she slept peacefully with no invading notions of Claire's problems or Applebee's mystery anywhere in her thoughts. Tonight, her thoughts were only of Nathan and a fantasy relationship she'd been having for years.

The next morning Nathan and Nina both arose earlier than expected. Nina went directly to Claire's office and pulled the manuscript out of the drawer. She wanted to make a copy of it so she could read it when she arrived home. Going down to the kitchen to find Nathan, she asked him if they could stop someplace on the way to the airport to get a copy made. He brushed her off and told her he would take care of it and mail it to her. She coaxed him to change his mind because she wanted to read it on the plane, but ended up handing it to Nathan, hoping he wouldn't think she felt too strongly about it. To alleviate her distress, Nathan 'offered to buy her a magazine before she got on the plane.

They left exactly at eleven and, as promised, Nathan drove Nina to the cemetery to say her final goodbyes to Claire. When Nina got out of the car at the cemetery, she felt the weight of Nathan's eyes on her. Slowly approaching the gravesite she noticing there were still many bouquets of flowers resting there—a testament to how many people cared for Claire and Nathan. Without realizing it, Nina whispered softly, as if Claire was actually there and could hear her, "I'm truly sorry about how things turned out. I hope you understand, Nathan should have been mine from the beginning. He was mine in the first place. Now, it's my turn to be happy. Can you understand?" Nathan watched Nina intrigued with the fact she seemed to be holding a conversation with someone. "*Praying?*" he thought. *No, Nina was not religious. What could she be saying, and to whom?* He studied her closely finding her expression curious. Nathan resolved to say nothing to her in deference to her privacy.

Nina's flight landed on Saturday. It was nearly 8:00 in the evening. She woke early on Sunday morning and found herself following the same path she had taken with Claire years before. She was on her way to Applebee curiously excited. She wasn't sure if it was because she hoped to run into some of the old crowd, or for some other reason. Parking in the overlooking parking area, simply for nostalgic reasons, she exited her car and walked around the town just to see how much had changed. Everything looked the same, but nobody spoke to her, not even a courteous hello.

Nina decided to have a sandwich at the Afternoon Tearoom where she thought she would surely be recognized. She smiled at everyone and tried to look friendly, but did not recognize anyone. Still, no one uttered a word to her. Motioning the waitress over, she tried to engage her in conversation. She began thinking back to her first visit with Claire when they were introduced to Frank Smythe right here in this place. No such luck this time. All she heard was an apology, no offer to solicit anyone to talk to her. Well, at least the service had improved, it was fast and accurate, and the sandwich was good. There was still a group of gentlemen in the corner of the bar chatting, but she didn't see Mr. Smythe. She thought perhaps she would not recognize Mr. Smythe if he was there as the first visit was many, many years ago. Mr. Smythe may be rotund or bald or have any number of other aged appearances. Oddly, the atmosphere felt very much the same, only very different.

Nina was saddened by the thought that this place held so many memories for her, but seemed to have moved on without her. She was almost afraid to encounter Oscar and decided to head back. As she left the tearoom, almost as if lightning was striking, a memory flashed through her mind. She stopped and pulled her sweater close around her shoulders, as it enveloped her.

Oscar was questioning her unmercifully. "Why are you here? I told you not to come back." She was crying, disappointed he wasn't happy to see her. Nina asked Oscar if he would visit her, but he began to rant at her, his arms flying back and forth, his expression full of rage. She was sorry she had come alone. She felt threatened, and worried she might disappear never to be heard from again. All she wanted to do was run away, back to the safety of London.

Once the memory faded, she looked around to see if anyone had noticed anything unusual, straightened her sweater and continued her trek toward her car. She realized there was much about Applebee she had forgotten, gratefully so. Startled from her reverie, Nina caught sight of Manny Legible coming from his uncle's home in the distance. He looked straight at her and paused. A chill ran up her spine and she jumped behind a large oak tree hoping he would not recognize her. She was reminded of the day she met Manny Legible, the newest doctor at the hospital where she worked. It was obvious he didn't know her connection to Applebee, but in a friendly effort to a co-worker, he asked her to go to tea with him. She had smiled at the expression she imagined on Oscar's face if she got involved with Manny and mumbled, "Maybe another time." She had turned and walked away as quickly as she could. He had not followed her or asked her again. She certainly didn't want him to recognize her here, in his hometown.

Feeling as if everything was closing in on her, she decided to make a break for her car. Taking a firm hold of her emotions, Nina walked across the square to the path to her car as quickly as she could. If anyone noticed she was making a run for it, they didn't say anything or try to stop her. When she got to the car she stopped, took a deep breath, and composed herself. As she got in the car, she realized she was just being silly, and didn't know why. Nina turned to take a last look at the village and without thinking much about it; she raised her phone and quickly snapped a picture. She attached the picture to a message and texted it to Nathan before heading toward home.

Nathan Burke was sitting at Claire's desk glancing through his wife's notes on Applebee when his phone chimed letting him know a message had been delivered. He opened it, excited to see a message from Nina. It said only "Applebee," with an attached picture. He opened it and sat staring at it in shock. Applebee was the village from the Constable painting . . . Claire's painting.

Chapter Two

NATHAN KNEW HE was not a sentimental man. Many considered him calculating, others thought he was seriously cold. But it had been difficult for him to pack up all of Claire's things. He had to keep stopping to gather his emotions. One-by-one he found himself revisiting the memories attached to each item. It was just all too final, yet it was a task he knew he had to suffer through by himself. Several people had offered to help, including Nina, but he knew it was his and his alone to do. He needed to see everything, to touch everything. He needed to feel closer to Claire, the woman he'd been married to for over 25 years, the one woman he truly loved. He didn't want any witnesses.

Nathan realized that when he returned to work, the time he had to figure out all the questions running through his mind would be limited. He labored for days over the decision to return to work or maybe he should retire. He decided on a third choice and requested a three-month leave of absence. In the meantime, he agreed to keep in touch. He rationalized that his position was important enough that he couldn't leave them hanging indefinitely. Nevertheless, the leave would give him time to decide if he wanted to stay in the home he shared with

Claire or find a new place to call home. It would give him time to decide if work was going to be the answer or if he needed change. The big question was what would his life look like without Claire?

It had taken him two weeks to pack Claire's things up. Aside from a couple of special photographs there was very little of Claire left in the house, except of course the pit of anger he carried in his gut that reminded him every day that someone had to pay for what had happened to her.

Nathan had always been an extremely organized and deliberate person, so to anyone who knew him it was no surprise he decided to visit his old friend, Charlie. Charlie was the person who had recruited Nathan into the CIA from the military. He was a good friend who had been around long enough to know both Claire and Nina. He'd sort of hung out with all of them in London, until he was promoted to Washington, D.C. Charlie had been instrumental in Nathan being offered a position in D.C. as well, and he had always been grateful to Charlie for that. Without Charlie, Nathan may have pursued a military career, and who knows how that may have turned out. Charlie was, by educational standards, a psychiatrist. He possessed some very unusual talents that Nathan never understood or chose to think too hard about. He knew that, especially right now, Charlie was the one person uniquely qualified to help him.

Picking up the phone, he dialed. He waited patiently for Charlie to pick up. "It's Nathan," he said and then paused for Charlie's response.

"I wondered when you'd call. Are you alright?" Charlie was sincere in his question.

"No, not really." Nathan replied attempting to rein in his emotions.

"When are you coming?" Nathan wasn't surprised Charlie knew what he was planning. He never had to explain things to Charlie. He just seemed to know.

"I thought I'd leave tomorrow morning; I think I'll drive . . ."

"I'll clear my calendar. See you when you get here. Anything else I can do?"

"Not right now. See you tomorrow." Nathan hung up as a rush of relief flooded his thoughts. He was on the way to resolving things. Pausing, Nathan wondered why he had not called Charlie long ago. He made sure he packed the manuscript Claire had written, as he wanted Charlie to read it.

Because Claire had not been able to take care of their home for some time, Nathan had hired a property manager a long time ago. They made sure everything was kept up properly inside and out. As a general rule, even the neighbors were unable to tell when Nathan was away. Today's electronic capabilities were amazing, and Nathan had made it his mission to keep up on the latest trade trends. Nobody handled his finances except him, he didn't trust anyone that much! He figured if he paid for a job that was acceptable. Even though he had an investment counselor, he chose to keep up with his own finances. After all, in his profession, he was apt to know more about unstable markets before the Wall Street guys.

On the other hand, Charlie had retired from the CIA about three years ago when a favor for a friend turned into a sort of full-time job. It provided a secure income with half the risk. Charlie had always wanted to be his own boss with a fancy office in downtown Manhattan. Not too shabby for a retired government operative. He'd definitely been in worse. Just being in the building had gotten him a few smaller clients and of course the CIA still called him when they had a certain type of "case" for which they knew Charlie was especially suited.

Charlie had hired an ex-marine as his personal secretary. Her name was Janola but she preferred to be called Lola. She was a bottle blonde with a big rack, looking as if she stepped off a stage at a sideshow. She was too old and out of shape for active duty but not old enough to collect social security. Nathan was impressed that Lola had, at one time, had top-secret clearance as it meant she could keep her mouth shut and in this business that could be critical. Charlie trusted her explicitly and loved that she had this way of letting clients think she was a dumb blonde incapable of being a threat. Thus, they mistakenly felt free to talk around her. More than once, she had been able to give Charlie information the clients hadn't told him. Charlie knew she was worth the extra money he paid her.

The drive had gone well, and maybe had even been good for him. It had given him some time alone to clear his muddled mind and consider his options. Nathan arrived in Manhattan before 2 p.m. and called Charlie to make arrangements for lunch. They agreed to meet at a 50s style diner around the corner from where Charlie lived. Charlie went there frequently and knew they could talk as long as they wanted with plenty of hot coffee. They spent an hour catching up on friends; several had died, a few retired, and a couple just seemed to disappear—they both understood the implications of that.

Eventually, Charlie asked the big question, "How did Claire die, Nathan?" Nathan's mind went back to a time when Charlie and Claire had been friends. He smiled at the memory of how jealous he'd been and was sure if he hadn't swept Claire off her feet when he did, Charlie would have. "I'm sorry Nathan, I know it hurts." Charlie was sincerely sympathetic to Nathan's pain, but he had to know, and quite frankly he was a little hurt that Nathan hadn't called him to come before she died. He supposed he should have gone down for the services, but to his way of thinking, it was much too late.

"I'm still not really sure. You know she had something wrong with her brain, and they want to blame it on that. But honestly, they don't know what that was." He paused then added softly, "I think she was murdered." Nathan looked up at Charlie as he continued to sip his coffee.

"What does that mean?" Charlie spoke softly encouraging his friend to share more, taxing his patience.

"The brain damage? I have no idea how it happened and neither did she." Nathan started. He proceeded to talk at length about how Claire changed over the years. He went into substantial detail for Charlie; hoping details may help him understand in that unusual way he did. He knew how much Charlie cared about Claire, and that Charlie would want to help. Besides, with what Nathan was planning, he needed Charlie to know all the details he could give him. He mentioned Nina briefly but didn't want to dwell on that part of the story. Eventually, he mentioned the notes Nina had found about Applebee and was surprised at Charlie's reaction.

"I remember that place," Charlie began with a little edge to his voice. "So, Nina was there?"

"You do?" Nathan's surprise showed in his voice.

"Yeah, don't you remember? Claire went there originally to work on an assignment from her editor at that rag she worked for." Charlie stopped to take a bite of his lunch and then continued, "She and Nina went there several times."

"Nina filled me in, a little."

Nathan shook his head not really understanding, but not wanting to let on.

"I can't believe Claire never told you about it." Charlie challenged Nathan's memory.

"I think she did Charlie, but I didn't listen. I thought she was being fanciful."

"She was excited about the assignment, and she worked hard on it. She wanted you to be proud of her, Nathan." Charlie didn't realize how deep his words cut into Nathan's heart until he'd said them.

At that, Nathan sat contemplating his friend's words. The realization that he had been so totally self-absorbed and had ignored something so important to his precious wife was a little more than Nathan could digest. He sat feeling like a naughty child being chastised. Finally, he spluttered, "It's horrible to realize you hurt someone you love and can't fix it. Can't even say I'm sorry," he voiced shakily.

Charlie nodded, understanding exactly what Nathan meant and feeling a little sorry for his harsh words. "It's not all your fault, Nathan. Claire didn't want you to stop her, so I think she hid things from you. I think she thought of Nina as a confidante, sort of like taking a friend along to share the experience. But I think Nina developed her own agenda."

"Why do you think that?" Nathan questioned.

"Well, Claire told me about working on the article, about the rhyme, and how she didn't want you to know until it was done. That sounded pretty straightforward to me." Charlie watched Nathan to see if he was following along, or if he perhaps had questions. "Nina talked about the people and the gossip surrounding that town. She seemed to be very interested in a few specific individuals, calling them her friends."

"And that was bad because why?" Nathan was having difficulty seeing where Charlie wanted him to go. Charlie's big question was if Nathan just didn't want to admit it to him or if he was actually that blind to the deceit.

"Well, Nina started to tell me she was worried about Claire, that the people of Applebee didn't like her very much—they didn't trust her."

Nathan still didn't seem to follow Charlie's line of thinking, "But they trusted Nina?"

Again, Charlie paused. "When did you ever know people to like Nina rather than Claire?" It was true. Claire was always the bubbly sweetie that everyone loved and Nina the mysterious follower nobody paid much attention to.

Charlie could see the light come on in Nathan's eyes, "So, you don't think Claire was hiding something like an affair." Nathan surprised his friend with the direct question.

"Hell no, Nathan. Claire would never betray you." He thought a moment then added an after-thought, "But I suspect Nina might have betrayed her friend."

Nathan gave a nervous laugh in relief, "So, you think Nina sold her out somehow?"

"Well, there was this one guy who I know for fact Nina got very friendly with. She told me herself that she didn't want Claire to find out. Said she'd be pissed!"

"Did Claire find out?"

"Not from me. But I always thought that was why the two girls drifted apart. Two very different agendas, starting in Applebee."

Nathan looked across the table at his friend, grateful for as much information as he had gotten and thought of one last question. "So, any idea at all what might have happened in Applebee that could have hurt Claire, but not Nina?"

"I've heard some rumors about Applebee but I never considered them reliable."

"What kind of rumors?"

"Crazy stuff, maybe witchcraft, or any number of other weird things."

"Nina was very anxious to take Claire's journal about Applebee back to London with her. I brought it with me, thought maybe you'd like to take a look with me. See if you find anything that might help."

"Be happy to actually. Oh, one weird thing, Nathan, you may be interested in. Annapolis just hired an intern from Applebee."

Nathan head jerked up at this information. "Really? What do you know about him?"

"He's an expert on ear problems, young guy, some big genius."

"How long is he here for? Do you think I could meet him?" Nathan showed his impatience.

"I'm sure it can be arranged." Charlie responded. "Maybe we could take a quick trip at the end of the week." Nathan nodded his head agreeing with that idea.

"I'm going to find out what happened to her Charlie. I'm going to find out who hurt her. And then I'm going to kill them." It was stated as a fact. Charlie said nothing.

Charlie had never married, so he lived in a one-bedroom condo high rise. It was elegant, with a spectacular view of Manhattan, but very small. Nathan decided staying with Charlie would be uncomfortable, so he took a room at a small inn nearby. As it was, the two old friends stayed up very late talking about old times. Nathan's mood improved as the good memories of Claire and the old days surfaced. He remembered why he had been so jealous of Charlie. Not only was he a very good-looking, athletic man, he was funny and genuinely kind.

Nathan would not be surprised if Charlie did not know more personal things about Claire's past than he did. They were both trained to notice details, but Charlie talked about memories of Claire that Nathan never knew. It occurred to Nathan how much Charlie obviously loved Claire. He'd always known he was attracted to her, but he never realized how deeply. He was glad he had not known.

Nathan arrived at the office a little after 9 a.m. He had Claire's manuscript with him, thinking Charlie could make a copy and help him read through it. As they sat over a cup of coffee, looking through the pages Claire had written, Lola announced a phone call from London. The two men exchanged surprised expressions and Charlie whispered, "It has to be Nina." He motioned for Lola to connect the call and clicked the phone for it to be on speaker. Nathan raised his index finger over his lips in a shushing signal to let Charlie know he didn't intend to let Nina know he was there.

"Charlie Lentz." Charlie announced as he would to any business customer.

"Hi Charlie, it's Nina." Both gentlemen heard the familiar voice.

"Nina Cavanaugh? What a surprise? How are you?" Charlie was good at playing his part.

"I'm fine Charlie. Missed you at the funeral."

"Indeed, I was sorry I couldn't make it." Charlie hid his true feelings about Nathan not calling him as he had obviously called Nina.

"Too bad, I would have liked to see you, Charlie." Nina's voice seemed sincere to Nathan.

"Me too. So, what's up?" He inadvertently rushed the conversation, as he might at the office.

"Can't a girl just call to catch up?" She pretended to be insulted.

"After all this time, Nina? I'm figuring you must need a favor." Charlie chuckled calling Nina on her deceit.

"Actually, I'm very worried about Nathan."

"Why is that? I've spoken to him, he sounded naturally upset at the death of his wife, but . . ."

"Of course, but he acts like he doesn't remember things. He says it was Claire who doesn't remember, but I'm worried it's him. His memories of London, before they moved to the States, are very foggy." Nathan's expression said he wondered what she was up to.

"Well, I'll give him a call one of these days, and see if I can get any feeling for how he's doing? Would that make you feel better?"

"It would Charlie, thanks so much, and give me a call back, okay? When are you going to come visit me here in London?" She plowed ahead without missing a beat.

"Oh, my job doesn't require international travel anymore. Next time, stop by and see me when you're here." The conversation ended on an odd note that neither of them really understood.

When Charlie hung up, Nathan asked, "Did I ever tell you, I met Nina before I met Claire?"

"No, you didn't," Charlie smiled devilishly.

"Yeah! Not my best moment, and I'm wondering if it could be part of the problem."

"What do you mean?" Charlie's head came up and showed his interest was piqued.

"We met at the USO, danced a few, and left to have dinner." Nathan paused a long while. "Then she asked me back to her place, which turns out to have also been Claire's place."

"Oh Lord. Did Claire know?"

"She never said anything."

"Why do you bring it up?" Charlie knew there was more to the story.

"Nina was acting a little odd after the funeral. I got the impression she was offering . . . if you know what I mean."

"Oh yeah, I know what you mean." Charlie paused and smiled "She hit on me in London. Asked me to "talk" one night, about Claire, so we did dinner, and then back to my place for the quiet."

"Did you . . ."

Before Nathan could finish the question Charlie continued, "Almost. We were into it pretty good, when the phone rang and believe it or not it was you." He paused, "I always wondered what turned her off . . . thinking of you must have spoiled the mood, I guess."

"I had no idea!" Nathan's shock showed in his voice. "Anything else I should know?"

"Probably a lot, Nathan. I get a feeling this girl has a plan, a very old plan that she's worked on very patiently. My question is what was her plan for Claire?" Nathan's expression showed he had not allowed himself to actually think that Nina could have in some way been responsible for Claire's situation. Nathan prided himself on being good at what he did. *How could he have missed so much?*

"So," Nathan continued, "Could I have been affected by the same thing Claire was?"

"How do you mean?" Charlie furrowed up his brow.

"Nina is describing me the same way I described Claire."

"Or is she covering her bases in case you call me?" Charlie suggested. "You have to quit thinking of Nina like she's another Claire. She's not, Nathan. You got the best of that deal."

Nathan sat deep in thought but felt compelled to ask the question again, "But is it possible?"

"I guess, technically, it is. First, we have to figure out what happened to Claire?"

The two men sat and talked about the details of what happened to Claire, when it was first noted, how it progressed, and decided that the key to the story was Applebee. Only Claire and Nina had actually spent any time there. "If my memory is correct Nathan, Nina and Claire told of very different experiences in Applebee, so I think we have to figure out exactly what those experiences were."

"I agree, so we start with Claire's notes . . . right?"

"Yes, then we can talk to Dr. Osborne. He may be able to help."

It was a beautiful day and Charlie suggested they talk at the golf course. Charlie was a member at Manhattan Woods, which was known as the premier golf club in the city. Charlie hoped the beautiful grounds would help them both relax. He knew in the pit of his stomach this wasn't going to be a quick case.

It had been more than two years since Nathan had taken the time to play a round of golf. As they rode back to the clubhouse in a rented golf cart, he shared his memories of trying to teach Claire the game, and how frustrated she got when she'd knock a ball off course into the woods or a pond. He had instituted the do-over rule, just for her, and told her how she needed to remember nobody else would honor the "Claire rule" as he called it. She accepted the favor and promised never to even play golf with anyone else, if they wouldn't recognize it. He had particularly enjoyed those times and admitted to Charlie how proud he was watching the other men at the club admire his beautiful wife.

After golf, which Charlie won easily, they stopped in the dining room for lunch and Charlie introduced Nathan to several of the gentlemen who frequented the club. This was not generally a military establishment, and most members were wealthy businessmen who were successful enough to be able to waste an afternoon playing golf whenever they wanted. As they were about to leave, Charlie saw a particular gentleman he wanted Nathan to meet entering for lunch. He waited until the gentleman had been seated and led Nathan over to the table where the man sat alone. "Dr. Harris, do you remember me, Charlie Lentz. This is my friend, Nathan Burke. Dr. Harris is head of biological studies at New York Presbyterian Hospital." Charlie smiled smugly at Nathan. "Nathan is a longtime friend of mine, Dr. Harris."

"Pleased to meet you sir." Dr. Harris rose and put his hand out to shake Nathan's. Both Nathan and Charlie hid their surprise at Dr. Harris' unusual way of speaking, each word pronounced distinctly in a deep almost cartoon voice.

"It is an honor to meet you, Dr. Harris." Nathan seemed confused why Charlie was pleased to run into this particular gentleman today.

"New York Presbyterian is the foremost hospital dealing with the developing brain. Nathan and I were just talking about a new doctor they have over at Annapolis, Dr. Osborne? I believe he works with the brain doesn't he, Doctor?" Charlie said by way of explanation.

"Yes, British fellow. Quite the scholar." Dr. Harris was probably in his early 70s, and quite rotund, but apparently, he kept up with his profession.

"He's working on something to do with hearing and the brain, isn't that correct, Dr. Harris?" Charlie coaxed.

"Yes, but I don't think that is really all of it. He's quite an odd fellow, conducts his work in private, very secretive. He's studied the Reicht diaries. Odd stuff that."

"Is it classified then? We wondered what could be gained with such a study of the ear?"

"He talks a lot about tinnitus. Maybe he's looking for a cure." Dr. Harris laughed. "No cure for Tinnitus, don't you know?"

"We're hoping to see Dr. Osborne about Nathan's wife, recently deceased. They've been unable to determine cause of death, something with the brain."

"Well, good luck with that. Osborne is very secretive. I'd suggest you try to make an appointment." Dr. Harris turned to Nathan, "But if you are in the military you should be able to twist his arm. Nice to meet you fellows." Dr. Harris turned and sat down to continue looking over the lunch menu.

Charlie laughed under his breath, "Guess he was done."

"Those brainy types, I've always found them a little odd," Nathan laughed.

"What say we get an appointment?" Charlie joked.

"Absolutely," Nathan imitated Dr. Harris. Then continued in his own voice, "In the meantime, let's do some research of our own, on Dr. Osborne," Nathan suggested.

The two men had barely finished their lunch when Charlie got a call from Lola about a client needing something. Charlie dropped Nathan back at his hotel and headed to his office to put out a fire. Nathan decided not to waste any time and headed to the public library to start his research. He found the New

York Public Library an excellent resource, not to mention its fascinating architecture. He spent the first half-hour wandering around just looking at the construction. He oriented himself to the layout, noting all of the exits, telephones, and restrooms, his CIA training always working. Eventually, he sat at one of the many computers with internet hookup and began looking for information about Applebee. The fact that he found one reference book with Applebee listed impressed him. The information contained in the book was so spot on he wondered how people could still be unaware of Applebee and its reputation. "Here it is, right here listed in a book in the New York Public Library," he mumbled to himself.

Applebee was less than 30 miles from London, on the river Thames. In 1920 it was well known for iron production. As he read further there was mention that in the 1850s a band of gypsies who were known to be reclusive occupied Applebee. The population was, at the time of the writing, about 500 people, up from the 379 that lived in the village 150 years ago when King George gave the land to Lord Smythe. The Smythe family still lives nearby in Castle Harleysville. It did not mention if Lord Smythe was a gypsy.

This information perked Nathan's interest and he began to search for information on the Smythe family. Apparently, although considered wealthy before, they made most of their money after World War I when the markets began to rebound. Their worth in today's dollars was over one billion dollars.

As Nathan understood the British system, Lord Smythe would be considered a sort of Governor or City Council leader to the town of Applebee. He was responsible for the residents, and they looked to him for political leadership. Nathan felt the Smythe family would be a good place to start, but his gut told him he needed information that couldn't be obtained at a public library before he approached Lord Smythe.

He was unable to find a reference to Dr. Anthony Osborne, but was not deterred, as he was certain "his people," so to speak, would be able to give him information on the good doctor. He looked at some books of maps to re-orient himself with the London area, trying to visualize his Claire driving from London to Applebee without letting on what was going on. He still had problems thinking of her as such an independent woman.

On a whim, he decided to look up the Reicht Diaries. He'd never heard of them. Unfortunately, he hadn't asked for a first name, so it took him quite a while to find Albert and Adolf Reicht. They were considered unreliable scientists. He supposed that meant mainstream science had not accepted their theories.

"Albert Reicht was a German scientist who suffered with voices in his head and eventually committed suicide. He complained that the voices spoke to him at such a volume he could not stand to be awake. In that era people assumed he had a mental disorder, but not even the strongest drugs helped quiet the voices.

Albert Reicht's son, Adolf, suffered from the same disorder but according to his personal journals, he suspected that the voices were actually brain waves being transmitted from certain people around him. He suspected the anomaly was caused by something wrong in his inner ear and thus he searched for a solution. Apparently, he had his ear drum removed in an effort to gain control, but the voices were still there. Adolf Reicht moved to the top of a desolate mountain to get away from people, but he too eventually succumbed to the voices. One sunny afternoon while out for a drive in his car, he apparently just drove off a cliff.

Adolf named the ear condition Reicht's Ear Anomaly Disorder or READ and often referred to himself as a 'Reader'. This confused the general public resulting in further isolation for the scientist as the public assumed he was claiming to be psychic, which at the time was tantamount to practicing witch-craft. The Reicht theories have never been proven.

The diaries from Albert and Adolf Reicht were part of an auction containing 14 journals, miscellaneous scientific equipment, and personal effects including Castle Glenveagh in Northern Ireland. The Castle itself was purchased by an Irish American art collector who in 1970 donated it to the Irish people."

Nathan was excited about all the information he was collecting, but finally recognizing he was getting hungry he gathered his research and stood up to leave.

As he was leaving the library, he noticed he had a text message from Charlie asking him to meet at his office in the morning at about 9 a.m. He stopped for Chinese take-out and made his way back to his room. An early night and lots of sleep actually appealed to him. If he were to get together with Charlie, they would talk and talk, and it would be past midnight before his head found a pillow.

Nathan woke early and decided to walk to Charlie's office. There was a little cafe on the way he thought would be perfect for a hot breakfast. Walking into Charlie's office, he was greeted with Lola's gravelly but cheerful voice "Good morning Mr. Burke, Mr. Lentz is waiting to see you, so go right in." Nathan smiled at her and tapped on Charlie's door as he opened it.

"Oh good, you're early. I have some people coming to meet you today, and I've made an appointment with Dr. Osborne. I called Sydney, you remember him. He arranged it, so it's all taken care of."

"What, were you up all night?" Nathan joked at how much had been taken care of and almost felt a little guilty that he had gone to bed early and had a relaxing breakfast.

"No, just got started early." Charlie smiled and held up the pot offering Nathan a cup of coffee.

"Sure, when's the appointment? Oh, and how is Sydney?"

"Friday. Turns out the guy is going to go back to England. Osborne not Sydney. Some problem on the home front, I think. So, I figured we'd best get to him while we can."

"Great." His enthusiasm showed.

"I've got someone coming in I want you to meet. I'm sending her to Applebee to sniff around."

"I thought I'd go," Nathan whined.

"Not when you don't have any idea what you're walking into, you're not an operative anymore."

Nathan sat contemplating what Charlie said realizing his idea hadn't been the smart thing to do. "When do we meet . . . her?" He was a little surprised that it was a woman.

"In a little while. She's worked for me for almost two years. She's good, just a little hot headed—trying to prove herself in a man's world." Charlie ended the sentence with a voice indicating some bravado.

"Do you trust her?"

"Sure, as long as you don't piss her off." Charlie smiled devilishly at his friend and continued with the story of their first meeting and interview. "She goes simply by Jo and pretends to be Russian, when in reality she comes from New Jersey. The one piece of advice I got about her from my contact was that she has a mean streak and doesn't mind getting rough with anyone who annoys her. I've kept her on a short leash, but I need someone who doesn't mind the unusual stuff, you understand." Charlie smiled at Nathan indicating he dealt with a lot of 'unusual stuff'.

Continuing he added, "I know she was interviewing me as much as I interviewed her. She greeted me with criticism about Lola, 'Couldn't I find one with a brain?' I ignored it and just motioned for her to sit down. It was clear that I had to take control of the interview. When I asked her about her last job, she went on for 10 minutes about how violent it was—like she was bragging. I know her type, and it took me awhile to trust her. She'll do the job." Charlie paused for a sip of coffee. "That was almost two years ago, she's done some good work for me since then." If pushed, Charlie would have to admit, he still didn't *actually* trust her.

As if on cue, the two men heard high heels clicking on the marble floor. They heard Lola shout like a drill sergeant at her to stop to be announced. They chuckled as it took a moment before Lola tapped on the door and gently opened it. She smiled sweetly at Charlie, winked, and softly said, "Josephine Frank is here sir, shall I send her in?" Lola was enjoying the extended delay and winked at Charlie when her boss didn't hurry to respond. Not uttering a reply, Charlie motioned for her to send Jo in. Lola stepped back still holding onto the door announcing in a soft calm voice, "Mr. Lentz will see you now." Jo walked past her with a sigh and then jumped as Lola slammed the door behind her.

Nathan tried not to look shocked as she entered . She was at least six-feet tall and looked like she could indeed handle herself. Her legs were long, and her waist small. She was wearing a very short pair of shorts with a matching waist length jacket and had on the highest heels he'd ever seen a woman walk in. Her light brown hair was severely pulled back into a tight bun. She wore a fanny pack around her waist and carried nothing else, at least nothing else he could see. She was actually quite beautiful, in a scary sort of way.

"Got something for me, boss?" Jo glanced at Nathan, waiting for Charlie to tell her who he was.

"Yes. It could be dangerous this time, Jo." Charlie spoke up right away.

"No problem." Pulling out a chair across from Nathan she sat down.

"This is Nathan Burke . . . Nathan, Jo Frank." The two nodded their greetings and Charlie continued. "Nathan is CIA. He has reason to suspect someone may have broken into his home and killed his wife. And, we think it may have had something to do with paranormal activity." Charlie paused to gauge Jo's reaction to this bit of news. He didn't think she would say anything, but he also would be surprised if she felt it was legitimate. As he expected she sat motionless looking back and forth between Charlie and Nathan.

"Okay. What do you need from me?" Jo was direct and Nathan liked that.

"Let's put it this way, I had a break-in at my home in Maryland. My wife ended up dead. She had not been well, but I had no reason to believe she was dying." Nathan paused, "I want to find out what happened and take care of it."

"Was anything stolen?" Jo replied pausing, cautious not to anger Charlie.

"I don't think so."

"Charlie . . ." Charlie recognized her whine.

"Claire and Nathan are very good friends of mine, and I told you Nathan is CIA. I trust his word, completely." Before she could say more, he continued, "I feel certain there are unnatural forces at work here. I know you don't believe in them, but you also know I have significant experience on my side. If you don't want the job, I will find someone else, but I'd rather have you on this case."

"What do you mean? I mean really! When you say unnatural forces?" Jo crossed her legs like a man would as if to challenge Charlie's control.

"I mean things we don't understand. Dangerous things."

She turned to Nathan, "What do you think may have happened to her?"

Charlie answered before Nathan could, "We don't know for sure. We are going to DC to question someone who may have some answers. Oh, and I need you to hire someone who will have your back. The job starts in England."

She smiled slyly; obviously happy with the thought she would get to travel. She asked for details about the personal circumstances of a second person, and Charlie handed her an envelope. "While we get a few answers, you find your second. Deal?"

She was checking out the envelope and nodded.

"We'll see you and your second back here in a week. Oh, and Jo, hire a man. Someone with some muscle, someone intimidating." Sneering at him she headed for the door.

Private Michael Adams woke up in a strange bed, anxiously thinking about the last months of his life. He still didn't understand how it was his fault. He was the one who had saved his unit from getting killed. He didn't want to kill anybody . . . it was war. If it hadn't been for him, all of them, very likely, would have been dead or severely wounded. Following instructions was part of the military training he'd endured, but the chain of command bullshit had been his downfall. Supposedly, the blind obedience instilled in the training ensured that even the rigors and distraction of combat would not allow one's self interest to override the groups survival. That was his problem . . . he never did adapt to the all-for-one crap, always placing himself at the top of the ladder.

The end of his military career had come in the God forsaken desert in the Middle East where the desk jockeys had issued the command that was the proverbial back-breaking straw that killed the camel. Their unit had been assigned a "crucial" checkpoint on a road to nowhere. They were to monitor the occasional car, truck, or camel jockey passing by, but were specifically instructed to do nothing to "provoke or engage" the enemy.

On that fateful day, he'd been sitting on the hood of a Hummer, smoking a cigar, and daydreaming of a beach loaded with bikini clad babes. His reverie had been interrupted by a solitary figure walking toward the checkpoint all alone in the middle of the road. "Do nothing to provoke or engage," was the order of the day, but far from the forefront of his mind as he reached for his weapon and hopped off the hood to stand in the road as the robed figure got closer. His Lieutenant's voice interrupted his train of thought, "Marine! What the hell are you doing?" It was typical and should have inspired that instant attention-grabbing reaction expected of command, yet he'd remained focused, and noticed that as the man approaching got closer, he was mumbling something in Arabic.

Out of the corner of his eye, he saw the four guys that were playing poker around a makeshift table, and instinctively knew that their little unit was potentially being threatened. He raised his weapon and used the laser sight to find its target as he shouted, "Stop!" Then in Arabic, "Kaifa haloka!" The fact that he'd just asked the man "How are you?" was irrelevant, because at that moment he could only remember these two words were some sort of greeting. He figured it would get the guy's attention, but no such luck. However, he had gotten the attention of his buddies, and everyone watched as he continued to illuminate

the face of the hooded man with the laser dot that would assure
that he didn't miss.

"Marine, stand down!" ordered his Lieutenant. "I said,
Stand Down!"

Adams stayed focused on the approaching enemy. "An
approaching hostile, SIR," he yelled.

The Lieutenant walked past Adams then turned around to
get right in his face, actually turning his back on the enemy and
screamed one more time "Stand Down!" Before the Lieutenant
could grab the fore stock of the M-16 the staccato crack of
the weapon broke the silence of the desert, echoing across the
emptiness as everyone observed the nearly headless figure only
yards away drop to the dusty roadway. Seconds later, the dead
figure erupted in fire as the explosion from the bomb he carried
consumed all three men. It would later be determined that
Private Adams was not killed because the Lieutenant's body had
taken the brunt of the blast and thus had protected him.

After three months in a Navy prison hospital, facing charges
of insubordination, Adams was dishonorably discharged. The
four soldiers who were playing cards testified that indeed
Adams had disobeyed a direct order, causing the Lieutenant to
lose focus on the approaching enemy. This incident, in addition
to a history of problems conforming to orders, resulted in his
discharge. His unit stayed after the trial to thank him for saving
their lives. He appreciated that they apparently knew he'd done
the right thing, even though they testified against him. At least
they all knew he had saved their lives.

Adams worked for a maintenance company in Atlantic City,
NJ cleaning up at night. It barely paid for the cheap apartment

he had, but he could walk to work, and had a spectacular view of the parking garage, so he wasn't complaining. It was after his shift, while he was sipping a cup of coffee in the café, "they" approached him. She got his attention when he caught her eyeing him. The once over told him she was his type, female. He figured she would be the type to strike like a snake if you angered her. He'd seen women like her before. But the upside was they were usually freaky between the sheets.

She approached him and introduced herself only as Jo and was all business. She asked him if he was looking for work, and he wasn't sure why, but he said he was. He was very curious about an immediate job interview that came to you, in a casino coffee shop. At least he didn't have to worry about arriving on time. She motioned for the guy with her to give them some privacy. "No threesome tonight?" He was always a smart ass when he was nervous.

"Funny." She sat down and the man with her walked past the table and stood somewhere out of sight. "So, are you interested in a job?"

"Working for who?"

"My employer likes to stay anonymous, but he pays very well." She paused, waiting for his reaction.

"Sounds illegal to me." He slouched back in his seat and flung his arm over the chair.

"And if it is?" she teased him to see what he might say.

"How dangerous is it?" he spoke quietly, and Jo smiled at him slyly, certain he spoke her language.

"There are a few conditions." He didn't respond, so she continued. "Don't ask too many questions." He nodded his understanding, "Follow directions, precisely." Again, he nodded. "Are you sure you understand? You don't question orders that get other people killed."

He leaned forward and stared into her pretty blue eyes in complete understanding of her comment. She had checked up on him, she knew who he was, so she had connections, "I'll do my best, but I won't die because the guy in charge is an idiot."

"Fair enough." Jo reached into her purse and removed a small envelope that she tossed to him before making her way to the door. Just like that, he'd gotten hired, and had a new direction in life. The envelope contained a cell phone, and a bank-banded packet of hundred-dollar bills. Attached to the inside cover of the envelope was a yellow sticky note with a handwritten message. It simply read, "Will call you. Buy a suit."

Chapter Three

CHARLIE AND NATHAN both rose early Friday morning and met for a good breakfast at the diner. They were planning to set out late in the morning for Annapolis. Charlie had made reservations at a hotel used frequently by guests visiting the CIA. The two wanted to check in before their appointment with Doctor Osborne, which was scheduled for early afternoon.

Arriving at Doctor Osborne's office a little early they found it locked up tight. As the good doctor approached from the parking garage they were lounging against the wall across from his door. It was a natural part of their training to scrutinize him as he came around the corner. He appeared young and was quite tall and thin. He wore round, horn-rimmed glasses sporting a very short haircut, except for his bangs that drooped down onto his forehead, which aided his youthful appearance. His clothes served to complete the illusion of being from another era . . . a most different era. "Look, it's Sherlock Holmes," Nathan whispered under his breath.

"Odd," was all Charlie could think to say. It was difficult to imagine him being anything but a tall, little boy playing dress-up. "Dr. Osborne, I'm Charlie Lentz, I believe I'm your next appointment today. This is Nathan Burke."

Both men recognized the familiar accent as he spoke, "Yes . . . well, I'm sorry I don't have much time, I will be leaving day after tomorrow and I have much to get done before I leave." Dr. Osborne took a key out of his waist coat pocket and opened the door with his name on it. "Come in." They entered what appeared to be a laboratory but saw no office area or chairs. It was obvious Dr. Osborne did not intend to spend much time talking to them, and Charlie wondered if he was shunning them, or genuinely unaware of his faux pas.

"Yes, well, this is quite critical to us, so we appreciate any time you can spare," Nathan responded in a determined tone allowing no room to misunderstand their intention to talk to him today.

"What can I help you with?" Dr. Osborne set his briefcase on a table and briskly turned to face the two gentlemen. He crossed his arms in front of him apparently resigned to donating the time necessary to speak with them but intentionally wanting them to know he did so against his will.

"We know you are familiar with the town of Applebee, near London." They both noticed Dr. Osborne's eyebrows lift in surprise, his chin lowered in an involuntary reaction. Pausing, he eventually gathered himself, coughed, and a more non-descript expression showed on his face.

"Of course, it is my hometown." Nathan noted no guile, and his hopes rose. Having no notion that Dr. Osborne was part of any conspiracy or inappropriate activity, they had decided to approach him with honesty in hopes he would react in like manner.

"Mr. Burke was married to a lady named Claire who was originally from London. She worked for a tabloid newspaper in the 60s during the Vietnam war." Dr. Osborne stood patiently waiting for them to weave their story and make it of interest to him. Charlie continued. "Her editor assigned her to do a story on Applebee. She spent many days in Applebee investigating a nursery rhyme, do you know it?"

"Of course." Again, Dr. Osborne seemed forthright.

"Claire was a beautiful intelligent healthy young woman, until sometime after her visit to Applebee when she began to have headaches. We found out just recently, the headaches were a result of brain damage." Charlie continued stating facts in a non-threatening manner . . . but both men noticed as much as he tried not to show it, Dr. Osborne's eyes reacted to this information. "Do you know of any reason why her time in Applebee may have caused headaches or any other type of health problems?"

"There are many reasons one may get headaches and memory loss, of course. It could be as simple as allergies." Dr. Osborne began. "Is she with you? Perhaps I could examine her?"

"No, I'm sorry Doctor, my wife is recently deceased." Nathan responded, hurt with anxiety showing in his voice.

Dr. Osborne's eyes closed, and he bit his lip subconsciously while his head nodded slightly in a sympathetic gesture. Charlie felt the doctor's sincere feelings somehow changed things. "I am genuinely sorry for your loss Mr. Burke, but without examining her I'm afraid any diagnosis would be a mere guess. Did you take her to see a physician?"

"Of course I did. Several in fact. They felt that her brain had been damaged through an accident or possibly some unknown illness."

"And they did tests?" Dr. Osborne asked.

Nathan shook his head, keeping a tight rein on his temper, "Yes, several. They could not explain the damage they saw as anything natural or normal."

"Mr. Burke, what are you asking me?" Doctor Osborne took a more direct stance facing Nathan directly.

Charlie interrupted Nathan, "I think you and I both know what we're talking about, don't we? Charlie hoped to get a reaction from the doctor.

Nathan, unhappy that the conversation had gone in a direction he didn't understand, spouted, "I just want to know what happened to my wife!" His reaction had no effect on the two men standing face to face, staring at each other.

Finally, Charlie continued, "Things I don't think your community would want the U.S. Government poking around in?"

Dr. Osborne's expression was tight and thoughtful, and he turned to face Charlie directly "What are you saying?"

"You have a rogue, Doctor." Charlie spoke softly but with extreme malice.

"Absurd. From the 1960s? That was a long time ago, Mr. Lentz." The doctor's voice was strong and in control. He paused as if trying to determine the best course of action, realizing he would not be able to put Charlie Lentz off, "I will put you in contact with the right people. But, Mr. Lentz, I suggest you be careful. Some things will be protected." Dr. Osborne motioned for the men to leave, and they took the hint.

"A leopard doesn't change its spots, Doc. So, we'll hear from you then?" Charlie's words seemed almost friendly, the stress behind them.

"You'll hear from someone. I doubt it will be me." The doctor turned to Nathan with a slight bow, "Mr. Burke, I do wish you peace." His voice was soft and apologetic.

Charlie and Nathan left the lab and heard the door close and lock behind them. "What the hell was that?" Nathan stopped and looked back at Charlie expecting an answer. Charlie held his hand up suggesting Nathan hold on to his comments.

After they got in the car, with the doors locked and the windows up he turned to Nathan, "I didn't mention anything about memory loss Nathan. Did you hear what he said?"

"Apparently not. Let's get some coffee." Nathan had calmed down realizing they had found something. He wasn't sure what yet, but there was something. He knew he needed to keep his temper in check. He was too close to this case, and it was clouding his better judgment.

Dr. Osborne was an honest man, but even honest men have secrets. He was uncomfortable answering Charlie's accusations, not feeling that it was his place. He had a bad feeling that he knew what had happened to Claire, though he did not know who did what or why. If he was correct, a great wrong had been committed.

Charlie's favorite waitress just happened to be on duty when the two men entered the Defense Street Diner, a little place on the corner of Defense Street and Cedar. Just the sort of place Charlie liked. The waitress was the sister of an agent Charlie knew in Afghanistan. He had considered asking her out many times, but she had a chip on her shoulder over her brothers' death. He didn't really blame her, but he also didn't want to get into it with her. Her brother was young and was sent over too soon. He knew she blamed the agency, he would too in a way, but it wouldn't help her to know that he thought she was right. It might even make it harder. But she was still family to his way of thinking, so he always sat in her section and tipped her well.

"Martha, this is Nathan Burke, he's family." Charlie introduced Nathan to her unceremoniously. She already had the pot of coffee in her hand, sitting two cups on the table and filling them to the top.

"Nathan, good to meet you." She smiled broadly and Nathan responded in kind. He realized Martha reminded him of Lola, and thought, *I never realized Charlie had a type*. Oddly neither of the ladies reminded him in the least of Claire, whom Nathan knew Charlie had admittedly been attracted to.

"You learned more than I did from the good doctor, didn't you?" Nathan began their conversation with a direct observation.

"Apparently," Charlie sipped on his coffee. Sensing Nathan's frustration Charlie asked, "Do you want to interrogate me Nathan, or should I just tell you the story?"

"Talk to me, then I'll see if I have any questions." Nathan did not take offense at Charlie's snippy tone. Charlie nodded his head and sat back, getting comfortable. Nathan did the same, assuming it was going to be a long story.

"Okay, I told you after Claire finished her article, the girls stopped going to Applebee, at least so we thought. I don't think Claire went back at all, but she talked about the place quite a lot actually. Nina on the other hand did go back several times, and like I told you, she had a relationship with someone from Applebee that included him coming to her home more than once." Charlie stopped, waiting for Nathan to acknowledge his understanding. Martha came over to the table and the two men each ordered a sandwich. "You know that I observe people, I have a bit of a second sense about me."

"Oh, so you're psychic now?" Nathan snickered, realizing Charlie was serious.

"Call it what you want. I could tell Claire was struggling with her experience in Applebee. Her memories of the place changed as time went on."

"How do you mean?"

"When she first talked about it, she was excited and wanted to tell you everything in detail. What he said, what she said . . . but after a while, she talked about the stores, the river, and lunch. Same stories just less detail, no vibrancy, almost as if it had been erased."

Nathan seemed to connect with the description Charlie was painting and forgot his anxiety, "That's right, Charlie. It was like her personality was erased too. But if you noticed this way back then, why didn't we talk about it?"

"To be honest, with the trouble between her and Nina, and knowing about your attraction to Nina, I misread it. I thought it was a personal problem and didn't want to pry. I hoped she was just getting tired of talking about the place. Seemed reasonable as the months passed."

"My attraction to Nina?" Nathan was surprised at Charlie's direct statement.

"I knew, Nathan." Charlie admitted. Then, before Nathan could ask, he added, "I don't know if Claire did for sure." Nathan's expression turned almost guilty, but Charlie continued before he could speak. "Then when Nina started to behave in a suspicious way about Claire concerning Applebee, I began to wonder. I figured those two were tight as they could be, but I was watching them fall apart."

"What do you mean, what was Nina doing to draw your attention?" Charlie was relieved that Nathan was actually trying to understand with fewer emotions.

"She had developed a friendship with a man from Applebee, and she acted as if it gave her an 'in' that Claire could not have, being married and all. She was proud to feel accepted and happy to point out Claire was not. She was almost excited that she thought they didn't like Claire, but they did like her." Charlie paused as Martha brought their sandwiches and asked if they wanted ketchup for the fries. Once she had brought the ketchup and asked if everything was all right, Charlie continued with his story. "She seemed real mean about it, Nathan. And if you think back, the two stopped seeing each other all the time about then. I know we were all busy, but I just knew it wasn't that simple."

"Okay, so Nina was getting some from a guy in Applebee, and you think Claire was jealous about it, and that made Nina feel superior."

"No. I don't think Claire ever knew Nina had a thing with some guy from Applebee. Claire was oblivious to all that. And I think Nina purposefully hid it from you." Nathan was shaking his head indicating he didn't understand Charlie's insinuations. "Do you know what Applebee is, Nathan?"

"A village outside of London."

"Okay, a village. What's special about it?"

"Nothing from what I could tell. It produced steel."

"In that library history lesson, did it tell you witches used to live there?"

"Yeah, in the 1800s." Nathan was exasperated.

"Do you believe in witches? Gypsies?"

"I believe there are people who call themselves witches, yeah."

"But you don't think they have any power?" Charlie was aware that their tone was getting louder and angrier.

"Their power lays in suggestion and fear. Not magic, if that is what you're getting at. Are you trying to tell me Nina put a spell on Claire and scared her into giving up her personality?"

Charlie sighed, "I thought you were more open minded than this, Nathan. Think about things like voodoo? Remember the things we saw in Africa?"

"That was not magic, that was torture. Plain and simple."

"Okay, let me get back to my story." Nathan continued eating and nodded for Charlie to continue.

"You know I claim to have a special type of ability, I know you like to laugh about it, but let's assume I do. My job with the CIA was as a profiler because I can tell them things about suspects other agents can't. And I'm right almost all the time. I don't know how I do it or where it comes from. I just do it." There he had said it. He sat still waiting for Nathan to react.

"If you were so important to them, why did they let you leave?" Nathan's question was a little more offensive to Charlie than he intended, but Charlie's response would change Nathan's thinking forever.

"Because they got some guy who is better at it than me. I introduced him to them. His name is Frank Smythe. He's from Applebee, and I bet he's in your wife's book." The two men just looking at each other, judging the others' reaction.

Deep in thought, Nathan wasn't sure what to think. He never really believed Charlie could do anything so unusual. He figured Charlie was especially good at reading body language and reading between the lines. "Tell me what I'm thinking." Nathan demanded in a low voice.

"It doesn't work that way Nathan, I'm not a mind reader!" Charlie shook his head in frustration. "But you're thinking you never thought I had any special ability." Charlie stated in a low tone almost as if his feelings were hurt that Nathan thought he was a party trick.

Nathan sat again for quite a long time staring at his friend. When he spoke, it was with a different attitude, "So, tell me about this Osborne. What was he thinking? What did I miss?"

Charlie was relieved that Nathan was coming on board so quickly. He wanted to find out what happened to Claire, and he didn't need Nathan to fight him at every turn, "He was thinking about how some people get hurt when other people 'observe' them." Charlie indicated the word observe in finger quotes to make his point then shrugged his shoulders, "Call it what you will, it's sort like 'studying' them, 'reading' them. Apparently, it is possible for people to get hurt in the process."

They sat reflectively pondering this new information. Both of them thinking about whether or not anyone would have hurt Claire on purpose, when suddenly Nathan blurted out with a tinge of laughter, "So, maybe you are one of these Applebee freaks?" Charlie's head snapped back, and he looked at Nathan, relieved to see the big smirk on his friend's face.

"You know I don't know where I am from . . . so it's possible." Charlie smiled back at his friend's shocked expression. The two men ate their food, satisfied to finish in silence.

The next day being Saturday, Charlie called Sydney on his cell assuming he was not in the office. Sydney was a small man, a book worm type, who was always sweaty, which is why Charlie never felt he could trust him. When they briefly told him about their interaction with Dr. Osborne, Sydney suggested he could work it out so that the doctor would not be allowed back in the country.

"What do you mean back in the country?" Charlie asked.

"He's leaving as we speak," Sydney informed them.

"We must've touched on something big. He wasn't supposed to leave until tomorrow." Nathan reminded Charlie of what Dr. Osborne had told them.

"Now wait a minute, we did a full background check on Osborne before we let him in. He was as clean as they get. His references were all stellar and from high up." Sydney, already sweating, was very animated wiping his face with a handkerchief, pacing around and mumbling incoherently. He apparently felt certain they would blame him for letting undesirables into Annapolis.

"Whatever that means," Nathan challenged the remark.

"I think we're talking about the pay grade." Charlie looked knowingly at Nathan who stood nodding his head in understanding. "So, Plan B then?"

They both understood why Sydney was not able to help them and they expected he would report every detail of what they had told him to his superiors. At this point the less he knew the better off they'd be. Thanking Sydney for his help, Charlie knew there would come a time he might need his assistance. Before Sydney could question them further, Charlie disconnected the call, hoping that Sydney would just forget about their conversation.

"So, it's up to you Nathan." Charlie recognized that since Nathan was still inside the CIA, he had the most to lose if they continued.

"I think we should try to talk to that Frank guy you told me about. Isn't he from Applebee?"

Charlie's eyes widened. "Why didn't I think of that?" Opening up his computer Charlie easily accessed a directory of offices for the CIA. Mr. Smythe's office was indeed in Washington. However, they would have to wait until the office reopened on Monday to call to request an appointment.

They spent Sunday reviewing Claire's journal. It was quite lengthy, and they couldn't help but feel there would be some kind of explanation in these pages to aid them in figuring out what happened to Claire. It didn't take long to realize this would be a lengthy project. As they read, they would stop and try to recall what was going on in their own lives at the time Claire was writing about. *It is challenging to remember specifics about a period so long ago, when you were unaware of circumstances of your routine life that would become critical events in the future,* Nathan mused.

Charlie was up early Monday morning so he could call as soon as the office opened to get an appointment to speak to Frank Smythe. To his surprise he was told Mr. Smythe had been called home on an emergency and it was currently unknown when he would return.

"Coincidence? I think not!" Nathan pounded his fist on the table, shaking their coffee cups.

"Let's go back to New York and get Jo started on her assignment, then we will go back to your house until Mr. Smythe returns. I'd love to see your home and we need some serious time to get into Claire's journal." Calling Jo he told her to bring her new muscle to his office on Wednesday.

During their brief conversation, Jo tried to get some additional information on what the job was going to involve, but Charlie told her there wasn't time to talk about it right now. He had caught her at a rifle range, getting in some practice. Feelings of excitement, anxious to get on with the job, and wanting to know more about what the job entailed put her adrenalin in overdrive. She finished the call as quickly as she could and went back to her place where she immediately called Adams and told him to get his ass to New York City immediately.

Jo spent the rest of her day doing research on Nathan and Claire Burke. She felt it wise to have an idea of whom she was working for. It was a more difficult task than she expected, she supposed because Nathan was still in U.S. intelligence and information about him would be classified. Even Bruce, her secret weapon, the guy who could always get whatever information she needed about anybody, told her it would take a few days and he'd have to get back to her.

Adams already had his hair cut, purchased a suit, and tied up a few loose ends so he would be ready, just in case. Now, he was glad he had. He couldn't remember the last time he'd felt positive about his future. He was eager to move into the next phase of his life, and more importantly, determined not to screw it up.

Tuesday, Jo was waiting by the luggage turnstile for Adams promptly at 4 p.m. when his plane arrived in New York. When she spotted him waiting to collect his luggage, she smiled thinking he looked pretty sharp in his new navy-blue suit with a high collar shirt open at the neck showing off some chest hair and a nice gold medallion. The suit fit just snug enough to show that the man worked out. But most of all she liked the way the pants fell off his butt and were just a little snug over the thighs. He had gotten his hair cut but it still hung over his collar and the five o'clock shadow set the look off very nicely. "Sexy," she whispered under her breath. He grabbed his bag and smiled broadly as he noticed Jo checking him out. He couldn't help but think how this job just might turn out to have some decent fringe benefits.

Having planned some entertainment for the evening Jo asked, "Do you want to get some dinner?" as he followed her into the parking garage.

He nodded and replied, "I need to get a room." She walked up to a sporty red mustang, got in and waited for him to stash his suitcase in the back seat and climb in beside her. She didn't ask him where he wanted to go, or if he had any money. Adams wasn't sure if she was trying to impress him or not, but her driving skills caused his respect for her to go up a notch. He liked a woman who knew how to drive a hot little car. Pulling directly into the garage of the Gramercy Park Hotel, after she parked in an out of the way space, she got out expecting him to follow her to the elevator. Hitting the button for the 17th floor, Adams resolved to just go along with the program.

The Maître d' recognized Jo as soon as they get off the elevator and grabbed two menus. "Right this way," he said as he half bowed to her and began to lead them to his best table. She said nothing, and just followed him to a table as she deftly slipped him a twenty. It was a beautiful table, against a half-wall overlooking the city. There was a glass ceiling that had been retracted making it seem as if they were sitting outside. Lush plants covered a trellis on the opposite wall creating the illusion of a private table. It wasn't completely dark yet, but bright lights were sparkling all over the city.

The waiter approached the table, ordering her usual, he heard her say, "and bring him the same thing."

"Usually I order for myself." Adams didn't quite object but he wasn't sure if this domineering attitude was taking things a bit too far.

"Just stick with me, tonight. I'll take you there, I promise." He wasn't sure he understood, but his gut told him she was coming on to him. Figuring he could afford to wait to see where this evening had in store, he simply sat watching her.

He really didn't pay much attention to dinner; there was only simple conversation. "Pass the salt, more bread?" was about all they said to each other. But at least the food was good and filled him up, not to mention free. It was some sort of BBQ meat with noodles and white sauce. He didn't really care. Gulping down his wine he realized he drank more than his fair share of it. When she was done, she sat staring into the distance until she was ready to leave. Suddenly, she got up looking back at him to follow like a new puppy. Adams rose deftly from his chair, almost annoyed, continuing to play by her rules. They walked to the elevator, and she pushed the button for the 13th floor.

"Where are we going?"

"My place," answering quietly and glancing over at him to catch his reaction, she continued, "It's your lucky day."

Following her off the elevator they stopped in front of a door just off to the left of the elevators and Jo reached out unlocking her door. She flung the door open and stepped inside. She tossed her purse haphazardly onto the small table just inside the door. Her shoes were next, kicked off and basically tossed across the room, and then she turned the lights on. Watching her closely, she walked across the room to the glass doors and stepped out onto a balcony. Pausing only a moment to look the place over he took in all the details of the room. Her apartment was a one room with a bathroom off to the left and a very small kitchenette to the right. The bed was on the left in the corner with a small sectional opposite to the kitchen on the right, and a very nice TV/Stereo was set up beside the glass doors. It was decorated beautifully, but he was unsure if it was her stuff or the hotel's. Looking up, he was surprised to find her standing completely naked on the small porch, still staring at the city.

She was completely naked! His mind playing with the phrase as if it was a foreign language. He began to eye her up and down, liking everything he saw. She turned and walked over to him, slowly. "So, do I need to give you instructions, or do you know what to do next?" He stood his ground and she stopped only when she couldn't take another step, her head tilted back inviting him to kiss her.

Reaching up he untied her hair. "So, are you going to eat me in the morning?" he whispered as his hands began to touch her skin.

"I don't think I'm going to wait until morning."

Chapter Four

THE NEXT MORNING Charlie called Jo's apartment from the office as soon as he got in. Jo was up, sitting on the porch finishing her breakfast while Adams was still sleeping soundly. "We are just getting started if you care to join us?" she heard his deep voice say.

"We'll be there in about half-an-hour." Getting up she quickly went to rouse Adams.

"We'll be waiting."

It took 18 minutes for her to wake Adams, let him eat breakfast, and rush him through a shave and a shower. She insisted he wear decent clothes to meet the boss. "You reflect on me, so if you want to keep this job, do what I'm asking you to do." He didn't mind, he liked to look good.

When they arrived at the office, as usual, Lola jumped up to announce Jo, while Jo did her best to walk by Lola in the doorway. Adams' entrance did not escape Lola's notice. Smiling sweetly at him she whispered, "I'm Lola," as he walked by. Returning her smile he reached out and touched her elbow whispering, "Charmed love." He thought for a moment she would swoon. Now, Lola had another reason to dislike Jo.

Nathan was reaching for a cookie smiling at Jo as she entered. Adams followed along behind looking much like her lackey, but when he saw the two men sitting at the executive desk, his back straightened, and his attitude changed. "Would you like a cookie?" Nathan offered the plate to Jo and Adams with a big smile added, "Lola made them, and they are spectacular!"

"She won't have one, she might gain an ounce." Charlie smiled devilishly at Jo who was making a face at the two of them. Reaching around Jo, almost as if to annoy her, Adams grabbed two cookies, then proceeded to a chair opposite Jo pouring himself a cup of coffee. Lifting the pot as if to ask Jo if she wanted a cup, she nodded yes. She was a little annoyed that he was making himself so at home so quickly.

Jo continued to casually stand at the desk and began to make introductions, "This is Michael Adams, the new guy. He's ex-military. She pointed her finger and said, "This is Charlie Lentz, the boss and ex-military. Nathan Burke, CIA, and ex-military." The group of them sat for a moment staring back and forth at each other amused that she could think of nothing else to say about any of them. When she finished, plopping down in her chair she waited for someone else to start the meeting.

Deciding it was best to stop joking around Charlie began by saying, "Welcome aboard, Adams. Nathan and I have a job we need you two to handle. I've already told Jo your destination is Applebee, England." Looking at Adams he explained, "It's near London." Adams did not flinch at the destination. "Things have happened that cause us to believe we need you two to gather some intel from Applebee. We're not 100% sure what will be involved. However, we do suspect it may be dangerous," he paused as he sipped his coffee.

"Jo, we found one name from Claire's book we suspect. Legible. They have been residents for over 100 years, and we suspect there's something really wrong with the family." Everyone sat patiently waiting for him to continue. "I think they may be involved in some . . ." Charlie paused hoping for the right words to express his next sentiment, "there's just no easy way to say this . . . supernatural things." Pausing once again while looking them directly in their eyes, Charlie tried to judge their reactions he needed them to be open minded, "I suggest you consider them very dangerous." Charlie reached over and hit the intercom "Lola, please come here, I have some things I need copied." In the blink of an eye, Lola came through the door, and Charlie handed her a file stuffed with papers. She took it and left again with an obvious glance at the cookies to see if they were being eaten.

"Okay, I'd like to know a little bit more than just there might be something wrong with this family." Jo sounded authoritative and Nathan wondered if it was for Adams' benefit. She had even pointed a finger toward him to emphasize her point.

Charlie looked at Nathan who had also noticed her demanding tone. Charlie chose to ignore it for the time being. If it persisted, he would have to speak to her. Charlie explained about Claire's newspaper article and her secret trips to Applebee. He explained about Nina and Charlie's suspicions that she betrayed Claire. And he mentioned his suspicions that Nina probably had feelings for Nathan, but that she also appeared to be involved with a man from Applebee . . . probably one of the Legibles. They explained what they understood about Claire's condition and possible brain damage and Dr. Osborne's reactions. It was a fairly complete synopsis. The only thing Charlie had left out was any implication that Nathan may have slighted his wife in deference to Nina or his past with Nina.

"I think I'm getting the picture," Jo remarked thoughtfully.

Charlie told them he had booked them into a hotel in London for two nights so they could do some local research to see if they could find anything interesting about the village or its residents. Afterward they were booked into a bed and breakfast in Applebee. Just then Lola returned with the copies she had made and handed the bundle to Charlie. He in turn handed Jo one of the files of information with specific instructions for them both to review the file carefully and not to take them to Applebee. It is critical no one see they had compiled such detailed information on residents or happenings concerning Applebee Charlie instructed. It also included airline tickets, passports, and cash. "Everything you should need, including two burner cell phones in case you get into trouble and need to call. You will be Jo and Michael Stevens," Charlie smiled at them.

"Really?" Jo questioned what she'd heard. She was thinking that she was just getting used to calling "Michael" Adams. So, this would be a challenge.

"Honeymooners, perfect cover. Most people don't like to bother honeymooners, so it should give you a little privacy from the locals," Charlie explained.

"So, you think there is some actual danger awaiting us?" Adams spoke up. "What kind of danger?" Charlie and Nathan were both happy to hear Adams sound as if he took the warning seriously. They both got the impression that Jo did not.

"I think these people will do what they feel they need to do to protect themselves," Nathan answered jumping in.

"And you think they are supernatural? In what way?" Adams asked carefully.

"Do you believe in supernatural things?" Charlie sat forward in his chair.

"The way I see it, there are evil things happening all the time. If there are good things, then why not bad?"

"Are you religious Adams?" Charlie asked.

"Not particularly religious, but it doesn't mean I don't believe in God . . . or in evil." Adams spoke in a way that told both Nathan and Charlie, he was intelligent and not just along for the ride. Charlie was relieved to see this in what he feared might be just a hired gun.

"Let me assure you, the evil in Applebee is in human form, but that is the worst form in my experience," Nathan opined.

Charlie didn't want either Jo or Adams to underestimate the situation they would be going into, so he offered a further explanation. "We don't really know what the danger is, but we believe it is done at least in part without the 'victims' knowledge of what is happening to them. That is why it is so dangerous. I also have reason to believe they can read your mind . . . I don't know how else to put it. Nathan and I are going through a journal his wife, Claire, wrote. Hopefully, it will give us some insight into what she encountered."

"So, what exactly are our goals in this investigation?" Jo asked.

"Get a feel for the place. Try to meet the people, especially the Legibles and Smythes, but don't get too friendly."

"Smythes?" Adams asked.

"Lord Gregory Smythe is sort of the governor in Applebee," Charlie answered.

"So, he'd be one of them, as well?" Adams questioned cautiously.

"I'm sure of it. But he's Frank's father, and I'd bet the Smythe's are the most trustworthy there. Of course, I wouldn't threaten him, I'm sure they'll protect themselves," Charlie clarified.

"What was it Osborne said? 'Some secrets will be protected'," Nathan popped in again.

"So, we're going to London." Jo stood indicating she was ready to leave.

When Jo opened the door, Lola was standing there. Jo stepped aside for her to enter, while remaining half in the doorway. Charlie and Nathan both wished Jo and Adams good luck, and Lola proceeded to shut the door behind them.

"Eavesdropping?" Jo shot back over her shoulder.

"No point." Lola held out both her hands to accentuate her apathy then added, "Have a good trip." In a sweet voice to indicate she knew all about what was going on. Lola smiled at Adams, and he winked back at her.

"I like her," he said to Jo.

Two days later, on Friday morning, Adams approached curbside check-in and saw Jo heading toward him carting a huge suitcase behind her. He stood motionless for a moment quite taken with the vision before him. She looked like a girl! He handed the porter a five-dollar bill and started walking toward his new bride. Her blonde hair was in curls, and she was wearing a pink and orange sundress with sandals.

"Wow, I like the new you," he offered as a compliment.

"Pl-eeeease!" she drew the word out to accentuate her attitude.

"No really, quite fetching."

"Like I care what you think." Jo handed the attendant the two tickets.

"Is that any way to talk to your new husband?" he said with a surprising gentleness in his voice. She chose not to respond, thinking he was baiting her, so he continued, "So, talk to me about our wedding . . . dear."

"It was freaking lovely. Why? Weren't you there?"

He glanced at her and sighed, "You are going to have to get into character, Jo. The people on this plane would be witnesses if anyone asked questions about our relationship. Might as well start now."

"You're right." She smiled up at him, but in her mind, she was marveling at how easily he stayed in character. She needed to step up and show that she was also up to the task. "Just like playing dolls."

"Oh, do you play with dolls?" he teased.

"Yes, they are named Smith and Wesson." She continued down the tunnel to the plane. Jo was disappointed they had been booked in coach. She was tall and felt squished with so little leg room. Adams was taller than she was with much broader shoulders and she wondered how he would handle it. He motioned for her to move ahead into their row, and then sat in the aisle seat beside her. He didn't seem to be bothered by the crowded circumstances. That annoyed her as well. Then, he reached inside the briefcase he carried and took out a book. He was planning to read.

"So, the honeymoon is already over then?"

"Why?" he said in a low calm voice.

"Reading? What do you expect ME to do?"

"Really? It's my job to entertain you? I gave you the window seat."

She turned as far toward the window as she could, hoping she would be able to fall asleep.

"I wonder if he booked one room or two at the hotel?" she thought out loud.

"Well, you can bet the Bed and Breakfast is one room, we're on our honeymoon." He said suggestively and smiled, enjoying her discomfort.

"Sounds good to me!" She turned around in her seat taking hold of his elbow and snuggling into his shoulder, "I've already tasted the candy and I won't mind seconds."

Adams made no remark to this lewd suggestion, but he smiled knowingly and turned his head and kissed Jo on the top of hers. They seemed to be calling an unspoken truce for the rest of the trip.

Their flight landed in London with no problems. Making their way to baggage claim, they gathered their luggage, and hailed a cab. The Washington Mayfair Hotel in downtown London was the perfect location for business trips when the point was to entertain and schmooze important clients. But when your business was in a nearby town, it didn't seem the best location. Jo had actually stayed at the Mayfair several years ago and was pleasantly surprised that it had been renovated. They had done an excellent job. It was an old hotel anyway and, if it was possible, it looked older than it did the first time she stayed there. Old and rich, a favorite combination.

The bellhop led them to their room, opening the door, he pushed the luggage cart inside. Lifting the suitcases off the cart he asked if everything was all right. Jo answered that everything looked wonderful then handed the bellhop a nice tip and turned to gloat at Adams. "Where's my room?" he asked after the bellhop left sounding like a 10-year-old. Without a word she pointed behind him to a closed door.

Jo continued, "It's a suite. I need to make some phone calls." Grabbing his suitcase Adams retired to his own room. Jo did the same and didn't come out until she had made all her calls and taken a short nap. Banging on Adams' door she asked if he'd like to go to dinner. Pleasantly surprised, she noticed that he had obviously had a shower and gotten cleaned up. They ate at a nearby restaurant, and then took a walk through downtown London enjoying the sights. It was good to be able to get some much-needed exercise. Before returning back to the hotel, they stopped in a little pub to try some British beers. There had not been much conversation between them until Adams asked, "So, should we discuss our plan?"

"We should. Tomorrow we'll do some research. Hopefully, we can find more information than Charlie provided. Did you have a chance to read the dossier yet?"

"Yeah, I looked it over carefully on the plane. What do you think of all this supernatural stuff?"

"I don't believe in supernatural stuff," Jo sighed.

"Not at all?"

"Nope. I believe in trickery." She sipped her beer and motioned for the bartender to give her another.

"I do believe." He looked at her directly as he said it. "I've had enough experiences to know there are bad things in this world that I certainly cannot explain."

"Like what?" she challenged.

Ignoring her question he said, "All I need to know is that if there is some crazy shit going on, will you have my back?"

"No man, or woman, left behind," she stated it as a matter of fact.

He nodded, "Dead or alive."

The trip back to the hotel was quiet, the serious overtones squashed any frivolous ideas they may have had, and they both retired to their rooms as soon as they returned.

They spent their first day at the London Library looking up everything they could find on Applebee, the Legibles and the Smythes. What they found fascinated them. The Smythe's writings were all about their leadership and community service. Their history went way back past anything they needed to know about, and apparently, they were richer than anything either Jo or Adams could imagine. The only interesting fact they found was how lucky they seemed to be always in the right place at the right time.

There wasn't much more information about Applebee other than what Nathan had provided them. They found more details about the area, and business history—things that were of little concern to them. There was a little bit more about King George having originally owned the parcel and his friendship with Lawton Smythe back in the 1800s. They couldn't imagine any of this was important, but it was interesting to note the level of associations the Smythe family enjoyed.

The information they found that concerned the name Legible was very different. An article taken from a London paper written in 1947, told the story of Oscar Legible getting into a fight on a ship while going from London to Paris. A man named Christopher Roles was with the crew and asked Oscar to step away from the banister for his own safety. No one really knows why Oscar became so agitated, but the two men fought. Christopher ended up bent over clutching his stomach and was rushed to the infirmary. There were no marks on the body, but Christopher complained of intolerable stomach cramps. The doctor supposed the man's appendix had burst. He was taken to a hospital as soon as the ship landed in Paris.

Oscar Legible was detained by the police pending an investigation. Two days later the man died. An autopsy showed the cause of death was that all of Christopher's internal organs were burned. They were unsure how they got burned inside, with no signs of burns on the outside of the body. The coroner felt the injuries were recent. Oscar Legible was eventually released for lack of evidence. No one saw how anything he had done could have caused the man's injuries. The death was listed as reason unknown.

Another report from a small tabloid told how Christine Legible had been expelled from the London College for Women in 1957. On three separate occasions, Christine was accused by different young ladies of coercing them to steal final exams. The evidence showed each young lady's fingerprints were found on locked file cabinets holding the tests. The cabinets were housed in the principal's office, which was always kept locked. Christine's fingerprints were never found on the cabinet but all three exams were found in her dorm room. The three young ladies were suspended until the next semester. Christine having had several misconduct reports on file, was expelled from school permanently. A follow up note stated, "The three teachers whose exams were stolen, each became ill and left school during the next semester. Mrs. Kindred, the math teacher, died. The police stated that although they suspected Christine might have played a part in this tragedy, they were unable to find any evidence to charge her with a crime."

And, most recently 1984 while away at school, Arnold Legible began stalking a young lady, Melissa Lennon, whom he apparently had a crush on. She spoke to campus police on more than one occasion about her concerns and the police placed her under increased security status. Witnesses say Miss Lennon told Mr. Legible not to follow her, that she did not want to date him.

Soon after, Melissa began to have frightening dreams involving her and Arnold in various romantic situations. The dreams became more personal and more real until she felt he was actually assaulting her. Her roommate indicated on more than one occasion after one of these dreams she developed bruises on her arms as if she had actually been physically assaulted or held down. On the night in question, her friends heard her screaming from her room, and woke her up. A doctor's examination showed she had been sexually assaulted. She claimed Arnold Legible attacked her. The police had gone directly from Melissa's room to Arnold's room on the other side of the school and found him in bed. There was evidence of sexual activity on his sheets, however his roommate swore he had been in all night and hadn't had any guests. No charges were filed and Melissa reportedly left school.

"Hey Jo, you have to read this one," Adams said pointing at the large book of newspaper articles in front of him. Jo put the magazine she was looking through aside and walked over to the table where he sat. He turned the book for her. The headline read: "Unexplained Explosion".

Jo read the article carefully with a suspicious expression on her face. "This can't be right."

"That's a newspaper, not a tabloid," Adams remarked.

"A four-story brick building exploded Thursday afternoon, with no apparent explanation. Fifteen people working in the building at the time are missing and presumed dead. Investigators have found no evidence of any explosive materials on the site and most curiously, significant rubble that should have remained on the site is gone." Adams quickly wrote down the address in hopes of visiting the site before they left London.

"I guess now we understand what they meant about super-natural, huh?" he smiled up at her.

"Give me a break. This is probably shoddy police work," Jo insisted.

"We'll see, won't we?" Adams said it almost like a challenge. "But I tell you what, we need to act as if these stories are true. We can't go in there all Rambo, y'know?" He was shaking his head letting her know he took this seriously.

Jo couldn't let herself believe any of this could be true, but she agreed. She didn't want him to think she wouldn't be able to handle herself. After a nice dinner at another local pub they headed back to the hotel. When they got back they decided to take a swim in the pool on the roof. It quickly turned into a competition to see who could swim the most laps. Adams swam much faster, and probably did twice as many laps, but he quit before Jo, and she claimed the win because she swam longer. Oddly, instead of the usual bickering that normally came after a disagreement, they shared a good laugh over their competitiveness.

Sunday, they were up early and checked out of the hotel. Adams made quite a fuss about another new outfit on Jo. She wouldn't admit it, but she loved the attention. This outfit was a pair of short-shorts, a top, and a vest, in various shades of blue. The long trim legs and blonde curls held back by a head band set off her look nicely. Deciding to have breakfast in Applebee, they rented a sporty, although very small car. Finally getting to see the place they'd heard and read so much about left them both anxious. Parking the car at the overlook they'd heard about from Claire's book they began walking into the town. Their first impression was that it was a darling little town. "Like a picture in a book," Jo remarked, impressed.

Just then Jo's phone rang. It was Bruce, her informant. She sat on the hood of the car with the phone to her ear listening intently to what he had to say. "Nathan Burke is well-respected, but the town didn't have a very good opinion of his wife. Apparently, she didn't socialize very much, and the women didn't accept her. Then, the medical examiner's report says she died under mysterious circumstances, and it sounded like they would like to lay it at her husband's feet, except nobody will believe he could kill her. Apparently, he all but worshipped her. They said she was pretty much a recluse for the last three years of her life. Oh, and get this, her maid says she is the sweetest woman ever. But then, Mrs. Burke left this woman $25,000 in her will."

"What about Nina, is she in the will?" Jo asked, and then added, "Did she have any money of her own?"

"No mention of this Nina woman at all," he said absent mindedly. "Sorry, it's not much, do you want me to keep digging?"

"Yeah, Nina doesn't fit. Check it out, oh and find out if there was anybody from Applebee, England anywhere in the neighborhood within driving distance of the house, on the night she died. And don't forget to check on the money." Her tone completely changed when she said, "Thanks Bruce . . . you're my hero." Jumping off the car she began to give Adams the scoop on what she had been told.

Adam's stomach growled and Nina laughed. It was definitely time to get a bite to eat. So, they decided on the first place on the left, Harrigan's. In an effort to play up the tourist angle and the honeymoon thing, they carried a camera with them and took pictures of everything. It wasn't anything anyone would question, a newlywed couple wanting to document their honeymoon, all perfectly innocuous. Harrigan's seemed a cheerful enough place. Although it was dark, it was decorated in rich, old English wood tones with expensive wood furnishings. They were casually greeted and given a menu. It seemed odd to their American sensibilities to get a whole menu for only two choices: A Full Breakfast of a fruit, eggs, bacon and toast or a New Breakfast of juice and cereal. It took a while for someone to take their order, but the food was generous and didn't take very long to be delivered to their table. When the waitress came back to see if there was anything else they needed, Jo spoke up, "I've heard there is a Duke living nearby. Is that true?"

The waitress looked at her for quite a while. Tilting her head she offered, "I suppose you mean Lord Smythe. They live up the road just a bit." She pointed in one direction, and then changed to another as if she didn't know which direction to point.

"Anybody else interesting live around here?" Jo asked and noticed the questioning look that came on Adams' face.

The waitress looked at them, unsure of how to respond to the unusual question, "Sure there are," she said in a simple tone, which made Jo wonder if she was special.

"It's funny how the village looks like it's stuck in time," Adams offered trying to sound intelligent.

"I guess. Most people here like it the way it is, so why change it?"

"You wouldn't want roads wide enough to drive a car on?" he suggested.

"Where's the traffic going to go?" She pointed out that the road didn't go anywhere. "We are a very small community, and it's much easier to walk or ride a pony without cars trying to get around."

"That's true, and very quaint," Adams stated smiling.

It was her turn to ask them a question. "What are you doing here in Applebee, today?"

"We're on our honeymoon and just looking around at secluded places around London." Jo offered, smiling and running her hand up and down Adams' arm in an endearing manner.

"Honeymooners, huh? There is another little village about a mile south of London called Thornton. You should check it out. They are set up for tourists and have a great little area where the locals dress up in time garb. Very festive."

"Thanks for that information. We might just check it out," Adams said cheerfully.

It did not go unnoticed that the Legible name never came up. They decided to check into their lodging and then wander through some of the shops to see if any of the locals were friendlier or maybe smarter.

After breakfast they returned to the car to retrieve their luggage, then headed to the Applebee Bed and Breakfast. It was a very large house that was converted into a charming hotel with a small restaurant. As they entered the foyer, a young, blond woman behind a counter greeted them with a big smile, "Hello, and welcome! I'm Millie, the hotel clerk, you must be the Stevens'." Jo and Adams stood smiling at this extremely cheerful young lady. She began talking and did not seem to want to stop. Taking the lead, as they walked, she explained that they were to stay on the second floor, right above a winding staircase. She described their room as having a lovely lavender hue, with white, antique furniture, at the same time showing them the towels, and how to work the shower. She asked questions, but never waited for an answer. Her very charming tour ended with her explaining that breakfast would be served on the hour in the dining room. Before she could get away Adams asked Millie a question about the town's history, to which she basically claimed ignorance by saying, "I haven't lived here very long. My mom and daddy were killed two years ago, and I came here to live with my grandma. We live outside Applebee a little bit, so I don't get to mingle very much with all the folks here in town. But everybody's been so nice to me," she paused for what seemed like a breath. Suddenly, she was gone out the door with a quick curtsey. Adams and Jo stood staring from the doorway back and forth at each other.

"Is she from South England?" Adams said quietly thinking Millie reminded him of one of those southern bells, except for the accent which was, of course, British.

Jo opened her suitcase and took out two shirts she had purchased for Adams. With her new wardrobe, she thought he should have some comfortable shirts to let the locals know that he is a tourist, because in a town so small new people wouldn't stick out without new colorful shirts. He couldn't help thinking these shirts were appropriate for Florida, not England, but rather than start anything, he decided to go along with the gesture and put on the least offensive shirt. He thought how he was really enjoying the sundresses she'd bought, but the shirts he could do without.

As they left the hotel's front doorway, they decided to go to the right and hit each shop in order so they could be certain they didn't miss anything. The first shop sold fresh produce and cold drinks. The proprietor there was an older man who was friendly and seemed harmless. He didn't even ask them why they were there. The second store sold ladies dresses and lingerie. It was operated by an old lady and her granddaughter. The older lady was a sort of busybody, telling them things about people they didn't know. It only took Jo a few moments to realize the lady was harmless and that she was telling the same story over and over, but changing the names to make it sound fresh. She supposed the lady was senile. The granddaughter was obviously there to make sure grandma didn't give away the store or hurt herself. The third store sold hardware. The proprietor was Jeffrey Binder, a father of twins. Jeffrey seemed like a hard-working young man, but with the three-year-old twins there, he could get very little done. They decided not to stay too long, as he had little time to spare, and either wasn't very talkative or didn't know much.

Walking around the hardware store toward what looked like a park, they noticed the entire side of the building was open and there were several horse stalls inside. This seemed unusual as generally the a concept went away about 100 years ago. People still riding horses inside a town seemed unclean, unsafe, and unnecessary. Taking Adams' hand Jo whispered, "Do you know if people in horse country, you know like in Kentucky, have horses inside the city? Adams stared blankly at her but did not respond. She supposed if people actually did ride from their homes into the town, it made sense, but she had not actually seen that happen before.

Jo noticed the pathway to the park went between the hardware store and the church, even though the church was set almost a full lot away from the hardware store. The side yard was fenced off, which made the distance seem smaller than it was. There was indeed a small park around the backside of the hardware store. The park fell at a rather steep grade to the water's edge of what seemed to be a rather large river. There were a few picnic tables scattered about and a couple of benches for people to sit on facing the river. Walking further into the park, they spotted a lovely bandstand pretty much hidden from sight until you looked back up the hill. Two couples sat enjoying their lunch at one of the picnic tables and one older man was quietly reading a newspaper down by the river.

Jo had walked ahead while Adams had been admiring the horses. He heard her call out for him and he quickly walked down to the river to join her. Strolling along the riverbank, they noticed there was an unseen paved road running behind the businesses. Adams reached out and took Jo's hand in a romantic gesture, then had to squeeze it to stop her from yanking it away.

"We're romantically motivated, dear." He spoke softly, for her ears alone.

She smiled at him and put both hands on his elbow rubbing up against him in a flirty manner, "Isn't it odd how so many things here seem hidden from sight. Did you notice the road behind the businesses?" she asked quietly. Adams looked up at the road casually as they continued to stroll along the riverside checking out the town layout. They would stop, every once in a while, and snap a picture or two with the camera. Jo was proud of herself for thinking to bring it. She thought it would certainly help them explain the town to Charlie. The streets had stopped, and where the streets would have been, if they had continued further away from town, seemed more like a forest, so they turned around to head back to town. It felt like a much shorter distance on the way back, and before they knew it they had passed behind the church and were facing a wall of bushes with a real brick wall behind them. The wall of bushes continued down to the riverfront and actually seemed to go several feet into the water virtually impassable unless you were willing to get very wet. "Vacationers probably would not push on." Jo whispered.

"True," Adams mumbled turning toward the water's edge but then continued to walk on. Jo followed along, wondering what he was planning.

"Where ya going?"

"Hey look out there." Jo caught up with Adams and turned to see what he was pointing at. The river appeared to be about half a mile across to the other side. But if you looked further past the point where they couldn't walk, there was a building on the other side. "Wonder what that is?"

Jo raised the camera to her eyes and began to focus the lens. "It looks like a still." She thought it seemed odd for her to think it was a still, since she had never actually seen a still. "We'll

89

check it out later," She offered, shrugging reaching for his hand. He led her back up the hill toward the church thinking it odd *she* took *his* hand.

At the top of the hill, they both noticed a raggedy old house behind the wall. It was on the other side of the church, but behind it, set back from the road so you could almost miss it. "Apparently, they like their privacy," Adams spoke softly, nodding his head toward the house to be certain Jo saw it.

"I'd bet it's the Legible house." Her face drew into a sort of smirk as if she felt certain she was correct.

"Can I interest you in some ice cream?" Adams whispered. As Jo's head turned back to look at Adams, she saw the little old man who had been reading the newspaper earlier walking up behind them. "I saw a sign for ice cream . . ." Adams continued as if he hadn't noticed the little man.

"That sounds wonderful," Jo said with more enthusiasm than she felt.

Suddenly, the little man turned and said, "Good Day." The man's voice seemed strong and powerful in contrast to his appearance.

"Hello," both Jo and Adams turned quickly acting as if they hadn't seen him.

"I hear you are honeymooning." the little man had actually passed them but turned to face them while he spoke.

"Yes, we are. Got married last Friday," Adams offered.

"How long are you in town for?"

"Just a few days," Adams again answered cheerfully.

"Odd place to honeymoon. Surprised you'd even heard of us." You could read suspicion in the man's voice that both Jo and Adams felt was unwarranted.

"A friend of the family, from London, suggested it. Said it was romantic."

"Humph . . ." the old man said, "What's romantic about it?" He turned abruptly and began to walk away.

"I guess because it's so cozy," Jo suggested trying to sound cheerful.

"We're enjoying it so far." Adams couldn't believe the old guy just kept walking, "You have a nice day, Sir," he said and held Jo back to let the grumpy old guy go on ahead.

They wandered up and stood on the street in front of the church, looking around the main street of the little village. "Where'd he go?" Adams asked.

"What was his problem?" Jo grumbled.

"I can't help but wonder if he wondered what we were doing looking behind the fence," Adams suggested. "Shall we continue?" He pointed toward the drug store, "Ice cream anyone?"

"What about the church?" Jo wanted to see inside the church. She had been thinking about it all morning. "You might say I have a feeling about it." As soon as the words left her mouth, she shook her head and headed toward the ice cream store. "Now, I'm having feelings," she mumbled. "First I predict a still, now I'm having feelings!"

"Let's leave the church for tomorrow." Adams pointed to the drug store, which is where he'd seen the sign for ice cream. Approaching the store, she looked back toward the other side of the church and stared at the raggedy old house set back from the road, with the same overgrown bushes across the front of the house. There was a walkway through the brush with an iron gate across it. They paused on the sidewalk, standing really close together and tried to look as if they were talking about something while they studied the old house. Something darted into the back of the drug store catching Adams' eye. Walking warily down along the side of the building he found another road running behind all the stores. Glancing around from back there, he saw more buildings off in that direction. Several buildings kind of like a small neighborhood, but not connected to the town. He sauntered back to Jo who stood waiting on the sidewalk.

"What was that about?"

"There's another road back there and a bunch of other buildings," he whispered.

Looking around the little drug store they noticed that they sold a variety of things, over the counter medications, lotions, much like what you might see in a drug store in the US. Jo picked up a map of the London District that said it included Applebee, and grabbed a candy bar. She spied some postcards stopping to take a closer look. There weren't too many, but she was excited when she saw several of them were of things in Applebee. She took any of them that were local and went to pay.

"We meet again?" There stood the little old man from the park.

"Indeed," Adams remarked not sounding overly friendly.

"We're just a small town, not a tourist destination," The man said in what he thought was an explanation for his behavior, but to Jo and Adams it was just more rudeness.

"So we've heard," Adams said dryly.

"We were looking for someplace where we could have some privacy on our honeymoon. We spent a couple of days in London, you know did shows and exciting stuff like that. Then came here for some down time, you know . . . privacy." Jo smiled trying to explain their motivation. "I don't understand how we're bothering you."

Adams marveled at the way Jo could sound vulnerable and noticed by the old man's expression her words had had an effect on him. "I know you don't understand missy, and I don't care if you get it?" The man was glaring at Jo with mal intent.

Adams was thinking what a regular guy would do, "Is the owner here?" he asked trying to sound annoyed.

"You want to tell my boss on me?" the reply was followed by some sinister chuckles.

"I believe you bring on yourself what you send into the world. And you are a grumpy old man." He wasn't sure if it was on purpose or part of the act, but Jo sounded like a hurt little girl having a breakdown.

"Come on honey, we don't need anything from here." Adams pulled Jo away from the counter leaving her items behind.

"We certainly don't need your business." The man turned and walked away as they left the counter.

Jo had a feeling the old man was staring at her, so she turned around quickly to look at him but didn't see him.

"Is something wrong?"

"We didn't get any ice cream," she whined then gave a slight smile as they began to leave. Adams pulled the door open, but just before she walked through it, Jo turned around and looked back one more time. This time she saw the man's reflection in a mirror hanging from the ceiling at the very back of the store. He was looking at her, and she flashed him a brilliant smile.

After the door closed behind them Adams said, "Ice cream? Did you really want some?"

"I don't eat sweets," Jo said as if he should know that by now. Jo didn't hear it, but Adams gave a big sigh of relief.

Exhausted, they decided to go back to their room and rest awhile. It occurred to Adams that Jo was acting a little odd. He realized he didn't know her very well, but she seemed vulnerable, and he wanted to be sure it was part of the act, and not something else. In the room she paced around the bed and then out of nowhere said, "I want to know if that guy is a Legible?"

Adams held up his hand to shush her, she hadn't noticed he was also walking around the room, searching it. She stood and watched him for a few moments wondering what he was looking for. Certainly, they hadn't given anyone a reason to question who they were, or why they were there. Adams stopped standing directly in front of her and stood silently with hands on hips. He kept making a gesture toward his ears.

"My inclination is to go get that little drug store guy and teach him some manners," Jo's anger rang in her voice. Again, Adams shook his head and waved his hand at her to shush her. He couldn't believe she was being so non-professional. He looked at her trying to signal her that he was playing his part, "Did he upset you that much honey? Maybe he was just having a bad day," he said in an obviously placating voice. She stood staring at him for a moment, and then seemed to catch on.

"I suppose you're right," she whined.

"Now, how about you get a nice hot bubble bath and relax. I'll get us some lunch from downstairs.

"Okay. That would be nice," she said thinking it did sound sort of nice.

"Soup and a roll okay for you?"

"Perfect." She went and started to pull a towel from the closet. Adams stared at her wondering why 'she was acting so odd? It almost seemed as if she was who she was pretending to be. "I'll be back in a few minutes with lunch."

Jo climbed into the tub full of hot water and added a few lavender salt cubes. Sinking down into the warm water felt so good she relaxed and fell completely asleep. About 45 minutes passed and Jo sat bolt upright realizing she had become quite chilled. She wiped her face several times, wondering how long she had been asleep. She had been in war zones without a flinch, but sweet little Applebee was messing with her mind.

In the meantime, Adams had gone downstairs and ordered lunch. Millie offered to bring it up to the room, but he insisted on waiting. He ordered the chopped steak special for himself, and vegetable soup and a roll for Jo. Millie suggested they would be having a dance over at the Cantina later, but he made excuses leaving her to think the couple wasn't interested. He thought he would have to get a bottle of wine for later, to play up the honeymoon angle.

When he returned to the room with their tray of food, Jo was wrapped in a towel, her hair was soaking wet. She asked him what had taken him so long. Glancing at his watch thinking he hadn't been gone for long, "45 minutes?" he said surprised.

"I think I fell asleep in the tub." She pulled out some clean clothes and returned to the bathroom to dress. He was stunned and sat quietly while they ate trying to figure out how it had taken so long to get the food.

"Time loss," he mumbled. He wanted to ask Millie if the meal had taken an especially long time to prepare, but he wasn't sure whether or not she could be part of this. *Could that be, sweet young Millie? Of course it could. And, Jo really is acting weird!* As he sat the tray outside the room, he decided to change his clothes to make it look as if they had both had a comfortable bath. He was going to have to be careful. He waited until they came and got the tray before he spoke to Jo about what she wanted to do with the rest of their day.

"I want to go see the church," she said standing up indicating she was ready to go and sounding much like someone who just wanted to see inside a church.

"Okay." He couldn't help but hope that maybe the church would be the safest place in town. He took time to set a trap on the door handle specifically designed so he could tell if anyone as much as touched the doorknob.

The church was only a five-minute walk from the bed and breakfast. It was Sunday, but way past normal service time, so when Adams opened the door, he found it empty. He paused, looking quickly around the church for anything that would help him discern the expectations or rules. He wanted to show the appropriate respect for the house of God. Seeing nothing to help him, he proceeded into the sanctuary slowly and quietly. It reminded him of a catholic church with kneeling benches and candles to light, and confessionals lining the side aisle. Being Catholic, he was comfortable with what he saw. He noticed how cool it was and the glimmering sort of glow from the candles. "Are you Catholic, Jo?"

"You know I'm agnostic." He smiled at the *routine Jo* response and paused to turn and look at her sitting on a bench seat, back straight, ankles crossed hands clasped in her lap. Although maybe a little nervous, she looked demure, feminine, almost vulnerable. Definitely different.

Walking toward her he sat down beside her, "You admit that in a church?" he whispered with a hint of a tease in his inflection.

"What are we doing here?" heeding his words, she leaned forward and spoke with a hush in her voice afraid someone might hear her.

"You wanted to come here," he spoke assuredly, without admitting he had been as surprised as she was.

"Me? To a church?" She had a most confused look on her face.

He stood up again and began to walk around to look at things. The pictures, vestments and everything looked like normal church things. Jo's jaw dropped in surprise when she saw him kneel down at the front of the church and seemed to be praying. When Adams stood up from his prayer and turned to face Jo, he saw a priest standing inside the door.

"Good afternoon, Father" Adams said politely.

The Father knelt in the center aisle and made the sign of a cross, stood, and then began to walk toward Adams. "So, you are the honeymooning couple from America? I'm Father Francis."

"Yes. Of course, you've heard of us. Big news in town." Adams stopped wandering around the sanctuary and stood facing the Father, a little embarrassed over his sarcasm.

"What can I do for you?" the priest questioned sincerely.

"My wife wanted to see the inside of the church. I hope you don't mind?"

"Your wife?" confusion could be heard in the priest's question as if he knew Jo was not Adams' wife.

Adams pointed back to Jo motioning for her to join them. "This is Jo." Adams thought the priest had to have seen Jo sitting in the pew as he walked right past her. He chose to ignore the question and continue playing his part. "How are you today, Father?" Jo came over quickly and held out her hand to shake the Father's hand in a somewhat gregarious manner.

"Nice to meet you, Jo," he smiled as he shook her hand.

"How old is this church?" Adams tried to think of a common question to ask and began to look around to avoid eye contact with the priest. He hoped it wasn't too obvious.

"It was built, at least this part, was built pretty much when the town was founded in 1677."

"Wow." Jo looked around "I can't believe it's still standing and in such good shape."

"Well, the addition in the back added plumbing and a residence for me. Otherwise, there is nothing to go wrong, it's just stone and mortar, with some wood furnishings."

"It's beautiful." Jo offered, looking around in an admiringly. Adams realized she was being sincere, and saw the priest smile with satisfaction. He believed her completely. "It has a peaceful feeling to it. Like God is here, right now," she said appreciatively.

"God is always here," the Father responded. "He is everywhere."

"Do you mind if we sit awhile longer?" Jo asked with a smile in her voice.

"No, the doors are always open. This is sanctuary." The Father responded and turned away.

Jo returned to her seat and sat back down. "This is the first time today my head hasn't ached horribly." Walking over to her Adams noticed the priest was still standing at the back of the sanctuary. He could tell by his expression the Father had heard her comment. Instead, he turned and left them alone. They sat quietly without speaking, both appreciating the solace.

When they left the church, they decided to continue their review of the shops in Applebee. The men's clothing store was next. The proprietor was a young man named Reginald Godfrey and probably the friendliest, most energetic man in town. Adams tried on an expensive jacket made of black leather. It fit beautifully showing off his wide shoulders and flat stomach so when Reginald gave him a 15% discount saying it was last year's style, Adams decided he had to have it, and would pass it off as a souvenir.

Since this guy was friendly Adams decided to talk to him a little and asked if Reginald had lived in Applebee for long. The answer was very forthright that he had only moved here about 10 years ago when his grandparents needed some help, so he moved in to help them out. They had since passed away. Then, he went on to explain that he had come to visit his grandparents here many times as a boy. His grandfather was a premiere leather craftsman, and as a boy he often worked with his grandpa making purses and bags. Adams appreciated the level of feeling this man had for his past, maybe even a little envious.

They skipped the grocery store but spent quite a bit of time in the bookstore. It was full of history books about England and London and the royal family. Most of the books looked used and Jo made a comment that it was almost a library. They sold coffee and cappuccino, and even lattes. "I wish we'd seen this before we drank all that regular coffee at the inn," Jo teased right in front of the clerk, and they all laughed comfortably together. It was a relief to know all the people of Applebee were not mysterious and frightening. The clerk was obviously not the owner, as she called the owner "Mr. Sigmund" several times. She herself was a young lady about six-months pregnant and overflowing with joy and expectation. "Mr. Sigmund is not in the store today. He doesn't like coming in unless nobody else can make it." she offered with no guile or malcontent, as if it was his privilege as the owner. Adams smiled at her lack of dissatisfaction and asked if she had any other children. The young lady, who said her name was Emma, answered, "Oh yes sir, this is my fourth." Both Adams and Jo were more than a little surprised, as Emma didn't look a day over 20.

"How old are you?" Jo blurted.

Emma smiled at the horrified expression on Jo's face and said, "I'm to be 29 next month."

"You're aging well with all those children," Adams covered for Jo.

"I believe it's because my husband and I don't eat meat. Can't afford it," she giggled just a little.

"What does your husband do?" Jo asked in a friendly manner.

"Oh, he's a farmer. Stays with the children. You know gardening, fruits and vegetables." Although they enjoyed chatting with Emma, they made their apologies for rushing off, but both Jo and Adams wanted to take a walk down along the river again, since it was the prettiest thing in the village. The afternoon sun was beginning to wane, and they each had purchased a latte along with something to read and wanted to spend some time enjoying their finds on a bench in the park.

"We met some nice people today," Jo stated as she pondered their day.

"Yes, well, they can't all be creeps," Adams said without thinking.

"No, I mean Reginald was really nice, and Emma was a dear. Really!"

"A dear?" He questioned her choice of words. "Yes, I suppose it is true. But Millie is very sweet, and that blacksmith guy was nice enough. The town is full of nice people. At least as far as we know . . . on the surface," he added.

"I guess, you can't tell for sure, but at least they were welcoming." Jo seemed determined to like them. Noticing it was getting close to sunset, they decided to change their clothes and check out the dance at the cantina after all. They should be able to pick up something to eat and party a little before bed.

They entered the front door prepared to greet Millie or one of the other desk clerks, but no one was there. Usually someone came to see who had come in, so they paused a moment, then went ahead when nobody showed up. Adams made Jo stand back as he pretended to put his key in the lock as he quickly checked out his trap. Sure enough, it had been sprung. Holding a finger up to his mouth he mimed Jo to stay quiet. As he slowly opened the door he peeked inside but saw nothing out of place. Entering the room, he headed for the bathroom, but nothing was out of place there either. Motioning for Jo to enter but to keep quiet, he pointed to the string he had used to set the alarm. He could tell by her expression she understood and was a also concerned.

They began to search the room methodically. Both of them went over the entire room. Jo found a listening device in the bathroom. Adams found one under the rim of the nightstand. It was nearly past dinnertime and they had to decide what to do. Adams went over to the radio on the nightstand and turned it on sort of loud. He returned to the luggage and pulled out a pen and pad.

I want to call Charlie, he wrote.

From here?

No. London.

Tonight?

In the morning. Do you still want to go to the party?

Adams decided to let Jo decide what she wanted to do since he felt certain she was being affected by something or someone in Applebee. Although he wasn't sure she understood that.

Do you?

I am hungry," he responded nodding his head.

Let's at least go eat," she smiled, ready to go.

Okay, but let's leave early, and get some sleep so we can head out early.

Good plan. She smiled at him, and they proceeded to get ready for their night out. It was obvious Jo was excited about going to a party. *At least 'I won't have to remind her to stay in character,* he thought.

The Cantina, as it was called, was just the back dining room of Harrigan's. The regular dining room was closed for the night. They put up decorations for various celebrations and would make the necessary traditional food, in this case Mexican. There would be music and the villagers would come, dance, and of course drink. Surely, it would be festive and loud so that no one would want to chat with them very much.

As they went downstairs and through the lobby, they turned around to see a few of the hotel employees dressed up in Mexican style clothing obviously headed out to the party. Joining in somehow they felt safer going with local people that had accepted them. To Jo and Adams' surprise, everyone drank heavily. Jo was pouring her drinks out, and only sipping whatever they kept serving her. Adams made the excuse he was allergic to alcohol and drank tonic with a twist. He said, "Alcohol turns me into an asshole." Everyone got quite a chuckle out of that.

The food was good, tacos, enchiladas, and frittatas, just about everything Mexican they could think of. The band tried to look and sound like a mariachi band playing music representative of Mexico with some rock and roll stuck in for dancing. The people of Applebee apparently liked to dance, and dance they did. It got late, and eventually, with Jo hanging all over him, Adams made their excuses, and the couple left for the evening.

Monday, they got up bright and early, got dressed, and went down for breakfast when the hotel restaurant opened promptly at 7 a.m.. There was nobody else around but a desk clerk they did not recognize and one waitress. Ordering light breakfasts, they ate quickly. This morning, since Millie was not around, they kept to themselves and didn't talk much at all.

Once they got to the car Jo began to talk more freely. "I hate this sneaky shit. I prefer you bring it straight to me; you know what I mean?"

"Let me remind you what these people can do," Adams remarked carefully.

"You mean *supposedly* can do," Jo responded with an attitude.

"I'm beginning to believe they can," Adams said as a matter of fact and began to back out of their parking space.

"Why?" Jo sounding more like her old arrogant self.

"Have you noticed at all how you are acting? Please tell me this is an act?"

The remark stopped Jo in her tracks. "Not completely. I wasn't sure you noticed."

Adams was surprised she admitted it so freely.

"I haven't known you long, but it's obvious you are not yourself," he remarked.

"I feel as if some other me keeps coming out, but I can't figure out why. I usually feel confident, like I can take care of whatever I am facing. But now I feel different, like my thoughts are not mine. Does that even make sense? Don't you feel it?"

Was she really feeling better just because they were on the road out of Applebee?

"No, not really. But I feel like we've switched places. I'm more taking care of you, than you bossing me around." He smiled smugly at her.

"That's true too." She smiled then slapped his arm before she sat back in the seat somehow a little more relaxed. A few minutes passed and Jo said quietly, "Oh my God. After two days I'm freaking out. Imagine what Claire felt?" The compassion in her voice spoke volumes. The rest of the way to London they remained quiet as they each reflected on the job thus far.

CHAPTER FIVE

CHARLIE PICKED UP the phone wondering why Jo and Adams would be calling when they well knew how dangerous it would be to have someone overhear their conversation. "What's wrong?" It had never been his habit to disguise his feelings and he wasn't going to start now.

Adams paused when he heard the gruff tone, and then looking over at Jo turning his back toward her to try and keep his conversation private. He doubted anyone in London would care what he was saying, but it was hard to drop the apprehensive feelings. He must have waited a little too long as he heard Charlie's voice again.

"Are you both okay?" Charlie's voice had changed to concern.

"Well, let's say this is more real than any of us expected." Adams didn't wait for Charlie to respond. "And it's having an effect on Jo."

"Jo? Really?" There was a very pregnant pause, "I didn't see that coming." Charlie's voice was more than a little surprised.

"I'm not sure it's a good idea to have her around Applebee," Adams whispered.

"Well, it isn't Applebee, you know that right? This is the work of someone . . . a person. The question is who?" Again, Charlie stopped talking and then continued, "Where are you now?"

"We drove into London to make this call," Adams whispered.

"Can you call me back same time tomorrow?" Nathan was gesturing frantically to Charlie wanting to understand what was going on. "Can you stay safe?"

"There's more . . ." Adams paused. "They're bugging our room."

"Who's bugging your room?"

"Well, I don't know specifically who. Someone from the village, I suppose."

"Why would they do that?" Charlie wondered.

"I don't know, maybe they don't want us to have a nice honeymoon, or maybe they need some thrills." Adams communicated his frustration sarcastically. "I don't know. Look, we've been really careful, playing our parts all the way." He settled down a little, not wanting to push too far. "But there is this one guy who openly resents us being there. He runs the drug store. I'm not sure who he is. But if they can read us like we think they can, he knows we're not who we say we are. I'd guess it's him."

"Okay, okay, stay there then. I didn't mean to sound like . . ." Charlie paused as he searched for a word.

"An asshole?" Adams said it with a joke in his voice trying to lighten the conversation. "Fine, I'll call you tomorrow." He hung up abruptly, looking over at Jo who was sitting with her head down on a table in a little outdoor eating area. Smiling at her he walked over to her and sat down. "Are you awake?"

"Is Pops upset with us?" Jo whispered, almost sounding drunk.

"No, not exactly. He's asking for a day. I'm supposed to call him back." He paused, "what would you like to do in the meantime?"

"Oh boy . . . let's go see Big Ben or the changing of the guard," Jo giggled softly. "I need to go to bed."

"It's nine in the morning!" Adams reminded her. It was obvious she was not in any condition to be walking around. He wondered if it would be too odd to drive back and then leave again tomorrow morning early in the morning. Yeah, that would be too weird. "I guess we'll get a hotel room." Another hotel room was outside of Adams' budget. He thought he shouldn't have bought the damn jacket and hoped Charlie would not mind paying for it. He did not want to drive all the way back to Applebee, and then have to worry about the bugs, and who knows what else.

Nathan and Charlie had been sitting in the office where Claire died, reading through the manuscript and talking about events from the past when the phone rang. Nathan waited as patiently as he could to ask what was going on. So, he didn't waste any time when he finally got the opportunity, "Well, are they in trouble?"

"Maybe. It's hard to know. He says they stuck to the plan, and yet someone seems to be watching them, bugged their room."

"Could anyone have known they were coming?" Nathan suggested.

"Who?" Charlie didn't think very long on the question.

"What about that doctor guy?" Nathan thought of one possibility.

"I guess he could have, but how would he know Jo and Adams were working for us?"

"Could he have read our minds?" That sounded dumb to him, so he continued, "Or maybe two Americans showing up right at this moment was too much of a coincidence?" Nathan suggested.

"When did we actually know we were sending them over?" Charlie thought carefully about what they knew when they spoke to Doc. "Wasn't it after?" Charlie replayed the last couple of weeks in his mind.

'I think you are correct. We spoke to Doc, then we called Jo to tell her." Nathan felt confident they had not made the decision to send Jo to Applebee until after they spoke to the good doctor. "But did you know what you were going to tell Jo when we were still with Doc?"

"This could give you a headache." Charlie tried to take some of the pressure off with levity, but instead it reminded Nathan of Claire's numerous headaches—years of headaches.

"I think we have to talk to Frank. He should be back today, and we need to lay it on the line with him." Nathan had some hope in his voice. Someone from Applebee, familiar with the place would be in a better position to know instead of speculating. Then he had a second thought and spoke hesitantly, "Okay, but what if he is one of them? Is that smart?"

"I think he would look at this kind of trouble as bigger than us interfering in their business. They need to know what happened, and I think Frank, well any of the Smythe clan, are decent people. I'm sure they want to control their radicals as much as we would. If these guys cause too much trouble, they could end up with international problems. He's going to realize that." Charlie realized he was rambling.

Nathan decided to rescue Charlie and smirked. "Yeah. Who wants to mess with us?"

"So, we play it as if we are concerned about his people too. We don't want to have to take action against this little village because a couple of radicals are running out of control." Charlie ad-libbed. Once Charlie made the call to Frank's office, they agreed they would start out for Washington first thing in the morning.

They continued with their review of Claire's manuscript until they had read it from cover to cover, but they understood it was convoluted enough that they were going to have to go back through it and try to digest it completely. "You could tell Claire was more scattered toward the end of the writing, and the story became more and more ambiguously written. There are lot of he and she references without being able to tell who he or she actually were," Charlie remarked.

"The article itself was not much better. It didn't go into any of the personal details the notes do. Sometimes she was like a child. Others, she was so scared and confused. All she wanted was for me to stay and protect her." Nathan said this in a monotone remembering those horrible end days. They were both determined to read through the writings again slowly and try to decipher what Claire was trying to tell them.

Charlie was coming to the conclusion that the article had been a basic fabrication. He began to wonder if Claire actually wrote the article herself. If they assumed the notes were the truth, then the article didn't make any sense. She had notes for an interesting expose but wrote nothing about it in her article. Slowly, Charlie began to read the manuscript out loud. He just happened to choose a part in the manuscript that was difficult for Nathan to listen to.

I had a big fight with Nina today. We were talking about her notion that she loves Oscar Legible and that he loves her too. I've spoken to Oscar several times and it is my opinion he is not interested in Nina romantically.

Anyway, one thing led to another and in the heat of the argument, she slipped and told me that she had slept with Nathan on the first night she met him. I tried to pretend it didn't hurt me that Nathan never mentioned it to me. But I had to save face with Nina; she can't know he's hidden it from me so totally. She would assume it was because of some lingering romantic intimacy remaining between them. Nathan would say it was because it didn't mean anything. So, I have to remember he didn't even know me when it happened. He would have picked her if he hadn't preferred me, and she knows that too. ✿

When Charlie stopped reading there was an uncomfortable silence, until Charlie finally began to read the next entry.

Nina is planning to invite Oscar Legible to her house for dinner. I told her that he is a dangerous man that I thought her being around him alone like that was dangerous. She told me she knows he is dangerous to me, because he doesn't like that I'm writing the article. And it's true, Oscar has not been very nice to me ever since he found out I was writing a newspaper article on the Applebee rhyme. But, as a newspaper woman, I can't let him intimidate me.

I came here today to ask her advice, in hopes we could bury the hatchet, but she laughed at me. Actually, mocked me. She said, "Finally a man that can't be swayed by your blond hair, big blue eyes, and innocent face." I don't understand why she's trying to hurt me. ✿

Nathan stood up part way through the reading, and walked to the doorway, standing with his back to Charlie. He said nothing at all, so Charlie continued on to the next reading.

It is Nathan's birthday and I already had a party planned, so I couldn't cancel it. I'd invited too many people to cancel now. I hoped Nina would not come; I knew she was still angry with me. I hadn't even heard how the dinner went with Oscar. Of course, she did show up. I heard the bell and when I went in to answer the door, Nathan was already opening it. There stood Nina making a spectacle of herself in the smallest dress I'd ever seen her in. Very low, and very short. She slithered up to Nathan slowly and sensuously put her arms around his neck and kissed him long and hard. She turned toward me and smiled so I knew the show was for my benefit. I turned to go back to the kitchen. She followed me and said she never should have let me have Nathan. Her tone was so a nasty all I could think to say back was, "What's the matter, Oscar not accommodating you?" She didn't answer me, but I really don't know if she actually heard me. I should have told her she didn't LET me have anything, Nathan chose me; pure and simple. But I was too angry to think straight . . . &

———

At this comment, Charlie stopped reading and asked, "Do you remember this?"

Nathan paused a moment before answering. "I remember that day very well. Claire had worked all day cleaning and making this really fancy dinner, while I was at the office. She told me she had a surprise for me when I got home. As I came through the door it was obvious she had planned a party. There were balloons; fancy dishes set out, you know, party stuff. We knew already that we were moving to the States, so it gave us a chance to say our goodbyes to our friends.

The doorbell rang, and I went to answer it. Claire was in the kitchen putting last-minute food in dishes. Suddenly, there was Nina at the door all wrapped in a coat, made up like a French hooker. As she came through the door, smiling wickedly, she dropped the coat revealing the tightest, shortest dress I had ever seen. I didn't even realize I was ogling her, to the point I was carrying a little wood, until she wrapped herself around me and kissed me, tongue and all. Almost knocked me off my feet. I really didn't think Claire had seen it. "

"Where was I?" Charlie questioned.

"That was the period you showed up late to everything, if you came at all."

"So, she did tell Claire she'd slept with you." Charlie observed Nathan's expression at his comment.

"Maybe that is why it wasn't hard to convince Claire to move to America. Nina was all she had, and I guess she didn't really have Nina anymore either."

"She may have felt if she didn't move to America, she wouldn't have you either," Charlie commented wondering if Nathan was beginning to understand all the levels of what he had been oblivious to.

Nathan picked up the manuscript staring at the page on top for a while before he spoke. "It would be nice to have Nina here to help us remember the details."

Charlie looked over at Nathan shocked , "Are you kidding? You still don't get it, do you? You shouldn't even tell Nina you're looking into this stuff."

"So, they had a fight." Nathan began to downplay what they'd learned but Charlie did not wait for Nathan to finish.

"You have to realize that it is very possible Nina was part of what happened to Claire. At the very least she knew about it!" Charlie paused as if trying to decide how far to go. "You know, maybe you should have stuck with Nina, and left Claire for someone who would have appreciated her." Charlie just shook his head and forced himself to stop his tirade, unable to believe this FBI agent, specially trained in espionage, would even ask such a question.

Nathan looked at his friend hurt, "You mean like you?" he shot back.

"Hell yes, me. If she had picked me, she'd still be alive."

Nathan didn't respond. He'd always known Charlie had a thing for Claire, and maybe he was right. Why did he always believe Nina?

Today, I was in Applebee for the whole day. Nina didn't come with me. I'm not really sure why. I told her I had an appointment with Oscar, and she said she didn't want to come. She always wants to come when I meet with Oscar. It was a cold day, unseasonably cold actually, and I arrived early. Applebee was beautiful. I walked down to the park and strolled around enjoying the breeze and the river, which always seems to have such fresh air around it. I guess my imagination was running rampant because I remember feeling like I was a character in a story. I was performing, pretending to be carefree, because someone was watching me. I heard birds chirping, felt the wind on my face and later sat in the sun until I felt at peace. It was the first time in a very long time since I felt so calm and free. Suddenly, I came out of my respite and realized time had gotten away from me. Sure, enough it was time to meet with Oscar. I had asked him to meet me at the tearoom, because I was leery of going to his home. Nina would say I am being over dramatic. I could hear people warning me not to go to the scary house behind the big churchyard. I couldn't help but wonder who would play me in a movie? I was hoping for Goldie Hawn.

I made my way to the restaurant and saw Oscar sitting in a big booth toward the back waiting for me. He stood as I approached, a gesture that surprised me. The past times we'd spoken I would not have termed him a gentleman.

"Gooday, Ms. Burke." His smile seemed sincere, but I couldn't help but notice his horrible teeth, yellowed and broken.

"Mr. Legible, yes, it is a beautiful day." I smiled back careful not to show my perfect smile. One thing I had always been lucky about was good teeth.

"I trust I have answered all of your questions?" He started out with an attitude already. But I was prepared for his lack of cooperation.

"Hardly all; I have a few more." The waitress came and I ordered the usual breakfast I ate when I dined here. We always ordered separate checks, as we didn't want to feel obligated to each other. "For example, why do I have a headache every time I have visited with you at your house? Do you put something in my tea?"

"Preposterous?" he smiled in a very unfriendly way . . . "It's probably because you have way too much stress in your life. As I understand it, your best friend is certainly not your biggest fan." I wondered why he would say that but before I could ask, he added, "Do you know where Nina is from? I've asked her but she says she doesn't know."

"I believe as she has said, she does not know. We met in a public orphanage when we were very young."

"So, it would be possible that she and I could be related?"

"I can't imagine how? Now, that is two questions for you."

Ignoring my statement, he reached into his pocket and pulled out a very old photograph. "This is my grand-mother." He paused as I looked at the faded picture. "Except for the styles, of course, she is the spitting image of Nina."

113

I reached out and took the photo and held it up to the light to get a better look. I was speechless. I had to admit, it looked just like Nina. Oscar continued, "My mother looked nothing like this, she was more like you. Anyway, my mother was expecting and traveling. She went to visit her mother by train. My grandmother was a mid-wife." He said this as a sort of explanation, then continued, "Unfortunately, there was an accident and the train was derailed. My mother went into early labor. Apparently, there was no one on the train to assist my mother with her injuries or labor, and she began to bleed heavily. She died. By the time the family was informed of all the details, we had lost track of the baby. I can't help but think that baby might be Nina."

I sat quietly for a while thinking how we could make such a determination. "How old would this child be now? Do you know where your mother died?"

"Twenty-six I believe. Somewhere between London and Leeds."

"I am so sorry, how horrible for you. So, this woman would be your sister?" I was softening with the knowledge of his plight, yet I knew I had to stay strong.

"My baby sister, yes," he answered with a stone-faced expression.

"Have you asked Nina about this?" I wondered what she may have told him.

"I have. To no avail," was all he would say. I wasn't sure what he wanted me to say when Nina refused to give him a satisfying answer. I was very sympathetic to Oscar's plight, but I couldn't bring myself to say any more about Nina's situation. I didn't really know anything concrete and wasn't sure if Nina wanted this man to know more about her. "I'm sorry, I can't help you. I just don't know that much about Nina's family or background. We were just kids when we met and at that age we didn't care about these sorts of things." I sat for a moment thinking about this sad situation, and then realized it was my turn again to ask the question I had ruminating in my mind.

As I started to speak, Oscar rudely cut me off. "What do you want from me? I don't have anything to say to you. There is nothing funny going on here. We aren't gypsies, we don't do magic or spells. We're just a small community that wants people like you to leave us alone."

His tirade was so embittered; he spat at me several times. I felt his rage in my bones. I sat quietly for a moment, and then mustered my courage to speak. I realized, as I spoke, many eyes watched us with surprised expressions on their faces. "I'm sorry Mr. Legible, but I am only asking a few questions about the legend of Applebee. Not about its current residents or magic spells. It's a public interest story, and we aren't trying to accuse you, or anyone else here, of anything. The fact you are so defensive about it makes it more interesting than it should be." Surprised I had kept my composure; I paused to gauge the effect my words were having on him and everyone else in the room. I saw a stubborn fool of a man who cared only for his own needs sitting opposite me. "Fine. I'm done talking to you sir and I will warn Nina to stay away from you as well."

Somewhat proud of my articulate rebuttal, I took money from my purse for my bill, threw it on the table, got up and headed toward the door. It felt as if he had reached out and grabbed my arm. I turned to look back at him and saw him still sitting at the table. I forced myself to walk to the door, even though something was pulling at me to turn around. Just before opening the door, I turned back and shouted, "You cannot stop me sir. I am free of you?" I ran to my car parked on the hill, got in the driver's seat, and slammed the door locking it immediately. I turned the ignition on *and as I looked behind me to pull out, I heard his voice "You will never be free of me." Certainly, I did not just hear his voice, I must have imagined it. Sheer stubbornness made me drive away.*

The drive home was difficult. I wouldn't tell Nathan; he would want to take me to the doctor and have me checked out. I needed to speak to the only person I could, Nina.

The next day I called Nina, but she didn't answer. I called again the second day and left a message for her to call me as soon as she could. On the third day I noticed a big black bruise on my arm where I felt Oscar grab me, even though I know he didn't actually touch me. As I looked down at my bruised arm, I became both horrified and filled with fright. I decided to walk past her house and see her in person. As I rounded the corner to her street, I saw 'them' sitting on the front porch, chatting as if it was the most normal thing in the world. Oscar, his little boy, and Nina on the porch, laughing. I couldn't talk to her now, not with him there. My emotions are in turmoil, I have lost my best friend.

———

Neither of the men said anything. The torment Claire was going through seemed way too real. "Are you remembering anything about this?" Charlie asked Nathan. "Even I remember some of it . . ."

"Goody for you!" Nathan mumbled sarcastically. Sitting quietly for several minutes, finally, he said, "I'm sorry Charlie. I should not take it out on you."

"Don't apologize. I understand what you're going through." Charlie actually did feel Nathan's pain. He also actually did remember some of this. Claire had spoken to him about the situation with Nina and Oscar. And Nina had spoken to him about her and Nathan. The question had always been where did Nathan stand, and today it seemed a more appropriate question than ever.

"It upsets me that Claire had to deal with all of this all alone. Especially, since it was my indiscretion with Nina that is being used to hurt her."

"Indiscretion? How was it an indiscretion? She understood what happened. Give her credit for that and respect her for not wanting Nina to get between you."

Nathan sat quietly pondering all the past events. *Should I have just accepted Claire's death and moved on*, he wondered.

Before he finished his thoughts Charlie piped in suggesting exactly what Nathan was thinking, "Maybe you'd just rather get in touch with Nina and pick up where you left off?"

Damn him, how does he do that? "I do care about her Charlie. I always have. But do I just feel guilty about Claire, because I didn't love her enough?" Charlie couldn't bring himself to say anything. Nathan's words filled him with anger, an anger he didn't have a right to. Suddenly, Nathan continued, "Okay the problem at hand is what do we do about Jo and Adams? Let's not get them hurt."

Charlie took a moment to ponder Nathan's comment, "Of course we don't want them to get hurt, but we also have to look at the bigger picture. Claire did not deserve what happened to her, Nathan. Because of what she went through, we might be able to get a handle on something potentially dangerous still going on. I don't think we want to throw that opportunity away. And don't forget, both Jo and Adams are Special Forces. They can handle this."

Nathan responded quickly, "I'm not sure about that. Adams is apparently worried about Jo. Do we know what that means?" Nathan was trying to focused on one problem at a time. "Do you think they are in real danger?"

"Could be," Charlie answered soberly. "Let's let it go until we talk to Frank Smythe."

"And leave them there for several more days?"

"I don't think we have any options. They can continue to play their parts. And I'll give them an out option, if they need it. Will that make you feel better?"

Nathan knew in his heart Claire would not want anyone hurt, so he nodded. Thankful they would have a way to protect themselves. "Without repercussions," he added.

"I can't promise that," Charlie answered soberly.

The next day, Tuesday, when Adams called, Charlie told him their decision. Jo was feeling better, almost her old self again. She insisted on going back to Applebee to continue the job. Adams made sure they understood that she began to get better almost immediately after they left Applebee. They all agreed she and Adams would stick closer together, and make sure they keep to their cover story completely. Especially anyplace there could be a listening device of any kind. Adams ended the conversation with, "I don't understand why they used a bug; can't they hear what we're thinking?"

Charlie responded, "Interesting point." The conversation ended without any resolution to the question. It made Charlie wonder if the point was to cause harm. Maybe these guys enjoyed being able to cause damage. It may be the only real power they have over people. It wasn't a pleasant thought.

Adams was also thinking what he could do to give them some leverage. He bought a CD player and a couple of CDs to play so there would be background music to help disguise the sounds in the room. Then he purchased a small dry eraser board so they could write each other notes without having to destroy any evidence. They went by the theater and dug through the garbage to get two ticket stubs so they could say they had tickets to a show. Then they did some shopping and bought a few souvenirs asking for an individual bag and tissue paper for each item, so it looked as if they had done a bunch of shopping.

Before they drove back to Applebee, they talked about how to disguise their thoughts when under interrogation. They chose a secret word (African Elephant) to let each other know if they got in trouble. They designed a plan for an emergency exit. Now, they were ready to go back. Being much better prepared, they felt much more relaxed as they pulled into the parking area at Applebee.

As they walked up to the front door of the bed and break-fast, they saw Oscar Legible standing in front of the drug store watching them. They made a point of laughing and joking with each other to make it look as if they were having a great vacation. When they went through the door of the inn they saw Millie at the counter, they paused a moment pretending to have problems holding all the bags. Acting very happy to see her, they greeted her and told her they'd be right back and headed to their room. Adams noticed the string had been dislodged from the door, so he made sure he went in first. As he opened the door his reaction was legitimate, he was actually stunned. He stood staring at the ransacked room as Jo stepped in behind him. Stunned, they both paused a moment, and at his nod Jo opened her mouth and screamed the best terrified scream she could elicit.

Millie and two men came rushing up the stairs to check on what happened. When they entered the room, they stood frozen shocked evident on their faces. "Someone has gone through all our stuff." Jo cried pretending to be nearly hysterical. It was all

Adams could do not to smile at her great acting job. He went over to her and wrapping her in his arms began to console her.

"Call the authorities!" Millie shouted down the stairs to her boss who was standing behind the desk. Instead, he slowly sauntered up the stairs to see what had happened for himself. When Millie saw him, she huffed, pushed by him, and went downstairs to make the call herself. Adams noticed that none of the others looking around their room seemed to have any intent of calling the police. It appeared as if they were only going to be looking around. In a few minutes, Millie returned and said one of Clarence Hopper's prize bulls had died and he was certain it was foul play, so the constable and the vet had gone to his place to investigate. They'd be by as soon as they were done at Hopper's.

Adams motioned for everyone to leave them alone. "Fine, we'll wait for them. In the meantime, Millie, could my wife have a cup of tea?" Graciously, she said she would bring one up right away.

While they were waiting, Adams began to look through the room to see if anything was missing, or more likely if anything had been added. Sure enough, he found another bug on the back of the mirror attached to the dresser, and one in the closet. Now, that made a total of four bugs. He shook his head thinking whoever is doing this must be hard of hearing. He took out a bottle of clear nail polish and began to spread a thin layer of polish over the tip of the microphones' surfaces. It wouldn't completely block the sound, but it would buffer it to the point it would be more difficult to understand anything they did hear, plus it would ruin the microphone. He smiled at Jo and said, "I like to play games too." He stated it as if he meant a different kind of game.

It was quite late when the constable finally arrived. Jo had actually fallen asleep but pretended to be very distraught when she climbed out of bed and put on a robe. Adams did most of the talking so Jo didn't have to over-act. He indicated several times how delicate his wife was. They seemed to understand what he meant and declined to ask her any direct questions. They did bring a technician with them to take fingerprints. This surprised both Adams and Jo.

The report didn't take too long to fill out since nothing seemed to be missing. "At least nothing we noticed." Adams kept saying. The friendly police officer tried to chat a little with Adams, but Adams didn't allow any conversation off script. The guy looked like he might have something in common with him, they were about the same age, physically fit, possibly ex-military, but Adams knew he could not take the chance that this guy might have some associations they did not know about.

"Any idea why someone would break in and not take anything?" Adams asked the constable.

"Oh, maybe looking for drugs," the constable suggested.

"Don't they take all that from you at the airport?" he chuckled but was in reality trying to decide if the constable was on the up and up or just dumb?

"One would think so. Well anyway, I'll file the report. I'm glad nobody was hurt." With that the officer was gone.

Adams whispered to Jo, "Odd he didn't find even one of the four microphones planted in the room?"

Jo sat up and whispered back, "I hope Charlie got the background right." She was obviously more than a little worried.

The next day, Adams went down to get coffee and a couple of muffins and asked if they could change rooms. Millie asked why and he said Jo couldn't sleep a wink in that room and he thought perhaps if they changed rooms, she would be able to relax. Millie thought that was a wonderful idea and told him the other room wasn't quite as nice, but it was empty. He took breakfast up on a tray and held up the key to the other room. He grabbed the dry erase board and wrote, "Now, they have to redo all the bugs!" Jo smiled and gave him a two thumbs up sign.

Taking their time getting dressed and packing up they moved across the hall. The room had about the same furniture, but the view out of the window was of the back alley. The restroom was little, with no tub, just a shower, and the closet was very small. Being nearly lunchtime, they decided enough time had passed for them to head out to continue their "honeymoon". Adams reminded her that he told them all she hadn't slept all night and was still not feeling well after the burglary. So, she put on her sleepy face and out they went.

As they came down the stairs, Millie was standing at the bottom with a wicker picnic basket. Adams smiled broadly and told Jo he had a surprise for her. He had rented a couple of bicycles, and they were going riding and were going to have a picnic lunch. At this Millie held up the basket and said, "I threw in a few extras, on the house, to apologize for all the problems yesterday."

"You are very sweet Millie, thank you." Jo went over to her and gave her a cursory hug. Millie giggled appreciatively and waved as the two honeymooners walked out of the hotel arm in arm.

"I thought it would be a good idea to stay out of sight today, so we are going to ride around Applebee's woods, and check out some of the other sights." He took her arm and led her toward the horse stable on the corner.

Nathan and Charlie were up early so they could be at Frank Smythe's office when it opened. As luck would have it, the secretary informed them Mr. Smythe had an emergency and would not be in today until 11:00 a.m. So, they decided to get some breakfast and asked her to make sure he was available when they returned. She smiled at their arrogance and told them she would inform Mr. Smythe that they would be back.

Upon returning at 11:30 a.m. they and found Mr. Smythe otherwise occupied. Charlie and Nathan both agreed the secretary enjoyed telling them this much more than she should have. Lucky for them he was also a punctual man and made himself available as soon as he noticed they had returned. His secretary announced them and Mr. Smythe met with them almost immediately in a conference room, instead of his office.

"You may remember me, Mr. Smythe, I am Charlie Lentz. I was here when you started."

"Of course, Mr. Lentz. How could I forget? I apologize for not being in first thing this morning. I am just returning from abroad and had some banking issues to take care of." Frank smiled over at Nathan and Charlie began by introducing the two men. Continuing, Charlie said, "My friend, Nathan, has a problem that he's hired me to help him with. In light of full disclosure, Nathan and I are personal friends. When we were both stationed in London, during the Vietnam war, we were actually in love with the same woman." Nathan's head sort of snapped to look at Charlie. He had never heard Charlie be so forthright about that particular topic. "Anyway, Nathan can tell you the specifics of why we're here."

Frank held up a hand and said, "Before you proceed, you need to know I have spoken with Dr. Osborne. I believe you met with him a couple of weeks ago?" Both Nathan and Charlie nodded their heads in the affirmative. "Dr. Osborne and I are lifelong friends as well. He was extremely concerned over your allegations."

"Over just the allegations!?" Charlie stated firmly. He thought it was necessary to ensure that Frank understood they felt the situation was much more involved than mere allegations.

After a moment's hesitation Nathan continued to explain, very briefly, Claire's history including some of the names of people involved. Frank's expression told them he knew the Legible family, which they expected, and he also reacted to the name Nina Cavanaugh, which they had not expected. He finished by explaining the long-drawn-out tale of the death of his wife.

Frank sat respectfully listening to the entire story. "Much the same as what Dr. Osborne told me. Can I assume some confidentially in this room gentlemen?"

Charlie agreed immediately, but Nathan had to make it clear he would not promise to protect anyone involved in wrongdoing.

Frank sighed and then spoke, "Mr. Burke, I understand you are an employee of the United States Government?" Nathan nodded and Frank continued in a low comfortable tone. "I appreciate your feelings about the death of your wife, truly you have my deepest sympathies. I would probably be more than determined myself. Let me say this, I believe it is possible that there has been some wrongdoings here. I am trying to get information about the situation as we speak. However, I have no evidence at all, and with no evidence I am not going to get very far." Frank got up and closed the office door. He pinged his secretary and asked not to be disturbed. "So, you are aware, I have given the United States Government full disclosure as well. Therefore, you are not hearing anything that is unknown. My situation is classified Top Secret, and I am aware you both have high clearances, but are *you* top secret?" He did not wait for a response. "What I am asking you is to keep my confidence, considering I do intend to help you. Can you agree with that?"

Again, Charlie immediately agreed, but Nathan hesitated before speaking. "Don't make me sorry," he drew his fingers through his hair and nodded his head in assent.

"Most of the people in Applebee are gifted with a sort of extra talent. We've known the perks of this for many years. However, in the last, say 25 years, we have also begun to understand that there are some unpleasant side effects. For example, I can tell you, Mr. Burke, that you are struggling with your feelings for one Ms. Nina Cavanaugh. You feel guilty over these feelings because they made you feel unfaithful to your wife. Shall I continue?"

Nathan shook his head no. He was amazed at the accuracy of the words and immediately began to think someone must have told him this fact. Frank continued, "No sir, no one told me anything." Nathan's jaw actually dropped slightly. It was as if Frank Smythe was inside his head. "Reading you is just the beginning, Mr. Burke.

"My mother is a 'non-reader'. After years of being around her every day, reading her at will and whim, we began realizing that non-readers who spend much time with readers end up hurt, with or without intent. I'm watching her drift slowly away because when we were young, we didn't realize it would hurt her. We scanned her to find out if we were in trouble, or what she got us for Christmas. She's all but gone today, so I understand your pain." Frank hesitated a moment to put himself back on track. Charlie and Nathan sat realizing this man understood far more than they initially thought. And now, so did they. "Obviously, this isn't something we want just everyone to know.

Nevertheless, we have some ideas of how to protect the public. This is what Dr. Osborne is working on so diligently, but his treatment is just not ready, yet." Pausing briefly to gauge their reaction he then continued. "Of course, we cannot hold our citizens prisoner, sometimes they travel. It is possible your wife was manipulated on purpose, hurt intentionally by some people who feel we, our kind, should have a larger place in the world. If that is the case, we need to take care of this."

Charlie piped in, "In deference to full disclosure, Frank, we have two agents in Applebee right now."

"Do you understand how dangerous that could be?" Frank got up and took out his cell phone. He walked away into another room for privacy. In just a few minutes he returned. I've just spoken to my father, and he is going to have them watched. Unfortunately, I'm going to have to go home to help deal with this. Apparently, they haven't been reported as a threat, but their room was broken into recently, which could mean something."

"But they are alright?"

"As far as we know, they are fine. Enjoying their 'honeymoon'." Frank smiled at Charlie.

"If you know you have these people, this type of people in Applebee, why don't you do something about it?" Nathan's voiced angrily.

"What would you like me to do?"

"What can you do?" Charlie reworded the question.

"That is a good question. Sometimes medication helps ... they are sort of like ADD meds, they don't really resolve the problem though. It merely slows them down a little, helps them control their behavior. Or we could turn them into a vegetable. Do you understand how hard it is to even incarcerate them? They are dangerous if they are angry or cornered. Isn't that also true of so many others as well. Drug Addicts, over-stressed people with sick kids. The guy who just got fired and has a gun, the guy celebrating with a few too many? Anybody who feels threatened, or cornered can be dangerous in many different ways. This is just another way." Frank sat watching the two men listen intently to his words hoping he was getting through.

"Okay, do you have any idea who might be responsible?" Charlie asked bluntly.

"I think we may, but we have no proof." Frank turned to his intercom and beeped his secretary. "Have them prep my plane, Marjorie; I'm returning home again . . . there will be three of us." Turning back to them, he continued, "We can talk on the plane. Meet me at the Washington airstrip. Do you know where it is?" Charlie and Nathan nodded. "In two hours?"

Charlie dropped Nathan at his hotel and told him he would be back to get him when he was ready. "I'll call you when I start back." Nathan agreed and went to check out of his hotel. The time flew all too quickly and when Charlie called to say he was on his way Nathan was barely ready.

As they made their way to the private airstrip Nathan elucidated, "Something's been bugging me. . . . He's got his own plane?"

"Why not, he's from the richest family in the world. I don't think anyone knows how much money these people have. Even them," Charlie quipped.

"How does that work? It just makes me feel so out of touch when I thought I was on the inside, and yet I have never heard of these people. It is pathetic that I don't even know who the richest man in the world is."

"Well, some, usually those with really old money, do their best to hide the fact they have way too much money. They act normal, even work. Maybe they just want to fit in, to feel normal," Charlie explained.

"And I thought I was doing well with my portfolio." Both men chuckled.

"The Smythe's are very cool about it. They seem like regular folks, until you pay attention to how they live. But don't ever forget money can buy most anything and if you cross them, they can make you disappear like that." Charlie snapped his fingers.

Looking up they saw a large black airplane coming in for a landing. It was given the highest clearance and got routed to the front of the line. Nathan remarked at the unusual black color and Charlie informed him that was sort of like a stealth airliner. "Apparently, they are concerned about being tracked."

He could tell by Nathan's expression he was impressed. "I guess they feel since money is not an object, they may as well be as invisible as possible, even when they fly."

"Especially, when they fly," Charlie reasoned.

The plane taxied to the terminal, where they saw Frank waiting for them. Three security men were standing with him. Nathan asked if Charlie knew why all of sudden, he felt the need for security.

Charlie responded, "Yes, he has as many security guards as there are often threats to his life."

"So, we are threats?" Nathan asked a little amazed.

"Possible threats. Don't kid yourself, we are not his friends."

"I feel so important," Nathan made a face with his comment. "How do you know all this stuff, I'm the one still in the CIA?"

"I was Top Secret." Charlie reminded Nathan, "And technically, with their capabilities, we are the ones in danger." Suddenly, Nathan didn't feel so cocky anymore.

Approaching the plane, they greeted each other quickly and boarded. Again, the plane was given top clearance, and in minutes they were high in the air flying exceptionally fast toward

England. Considering everything, Nathan thought the plane was nice, but it could have been much more elegantly furnished. The seats were very comfortable, and it was apparent there was a decent kitchen, but otherwise the amenities were scarce. It was obvious to him that the money was used to create an amazingly fast plane, not a fancy one.

The flight to England from DC would take nearly seven hours. Right after take-off, at about 4:30 p.m., they broke open a bottle of wine and sat chatting casually. The guards went forward in the cabin and began playing a card game. Their job was obviously on hold until the plane landed. Before very long, what started out to be reading and listening to music turned in to three sleeping men. The seats were extra-large and when folded all the way down, they made a nice, rather comfortable bed. Even the footrest rose so their feet didn't rest on the floor.

The flight attendant was an older lady and, perhaps acting a little motherly, covered each of the men with a light blanket and dimmed the lights hoping it would allow them to rest more deeply. It must have worked. For the three hours they slept, no one moved. When it was time, she returned, took the blankets, folded them carefully, and put them back in the closet. "We're about two hours out of London, Sir. Would you like something to eat?"

Considering the time change, it would be very early morning when they landed and since they had not had any dinner, a nice breakfast was warranted. The guards' card table had been covered with a tablecloth and a reasonably nice table had been set for breakfast. The fare included a delicious egg casserole, smoked applewood bacon, home fried potatoes, with a garnish of fresh fruits.

"Absolutely delicious!" Nathan remarked, rubbing his stomach wondering if he'd eaten more than his share.

"Very good, Smythe. Thank you." Charlie wiped his mouth with the napkin and smiled at the flight attendant as she removed his plate.

"Glad you've enjoyed it." Frank agreed with their assessment. "It was rather tasty, wasn't it?" He turned to the flight attendant and said, "Thanks Auntie, it was wonderful." She patted his shoulder as he passed.

The plane touched down, almost on cue, and they prepared to disembark. To Charlie and Nathan's surprise, they were not at the London airport. Instead, they were in the country as evidenced by lots of trees and the only building in sight was what apparently was a sort of very small terminal and tower. A stretch limo was waiting for them, and once they were all settled in, it sped off. Nathan and Charlie were genuinely impressed. Still, the view was nothing compared to what they would encounter at their final destination.

At most, the ride took all of 10-minutes. Pulling down a long driveway the limo stopped at a very large wrought iron gate held in place by large cement structures. Being security experts both Charlie and Nathan were checking out the place with green eyes.

The road leading to the estate wound around aimlessly and was lined by beautiful oak trees. The expansive front yard was effused with flowers that surrounded the grand structure. It appeared to be fenced on the perimeter, but trees and bushes hid most of the fencing. The driver drove to the back of the house into a large elaborate portico and they got out of the car and waited as the limo pulled away. An automatic garage door opened and the limo pulled inside.

Frank led the way up some steps onto a small porch. When the stepped onto the porch, the door flew open, seemingly by itself, and entered a sort of coatroom just outside of the kitchen. Frank led them down a hallway past what was certainly the front door and into a large office or maybe more appropriately a library. Upon entering the room they saw three other men resting in comfortable chairs. They all looked a great deal alike but of varying ages.

Frank shook hands with the man sitting behind the huge mahogany desk and greeted him by calling him father. "This is Nathan Burke and Charlie Lentz from America. Gentlemen, may I have the pleasure of introducing my father, Lord Gregory Smythe." Both Nathan and Charlie realized Lord Gregory Smythe was a man to be reckoned with. He was about 65, with grey hair and sparkling blue eyes. He stood and held his hand out to each man. The smile on his face appeared genuine, but Nathan wasn't nearly as comfortable with him as Charlie seemed.

Frank turned to the other two gentlemen who were still standing in front of their chairs in a formal gesture of respect for the newcomers. "My brother, Walter Smythe, and my cousin, Ashton Smythe." Both men stepped forward to shake hands as they were introduced and mumbling their greetings. All very polite. Trying not to let on he was uncomfortable, Nathan looked at Charlie noting he seemed very comfortable almost as if he were meeting old friends. Frank motioned to Charlie and Nathan to have a seat, and as if on cue, Walter and Ashton stepped aside to retrieve chairs for themselves sitting on either side of their guests.

Gregory nodded at Frank, who left the room to call for tea to be served. While he was gone the Smythe men chatted casually amongst themselves. This gave Nathan and Charlie an opportunity to assess these men they had just met, while they waited for the tea.

Walter appeared to be older than Frank, maybe 40 or so. A few inches shorter, sporting a little more girth with a little graying at his temples. It was obvious he did not have the charming personality that his brother possessed. Frank's mannerisms made you feel easy, but Walter was of a more serious nature and made you feel as though you had to be on your best behavior. His suit, probably hand tailored, let you know he had money and lots of it. Even Lord Gregory attempted to put forth a friendly air, but Walter seemed only to concern himself with his father's wishes.

Ashton was much younger than the brothers, probably in his late 20s, and easily the most attractive of the group. He was quick-witted and had a physical prowess that certainly would make him popular with the ladies. The sparkle in his eye spoke of a playful nature. His hair was dark blonde but had light streaks that appeared natural. One would assume he spent considerable time outdoors.

As soon as tea arrived, the conversation took on a much more serious tone.

"So, how serious is this?" Lord Smythe started looking at Frank to fill them in.

"Apparently Nathan and his wife Claire lived in London during the Vietnam war."

"Actually, I was stationed here, and met Claire here. She was English. We moved back to the U.S. a couple of years later," Nathan injected wanting them to understand Claire was English, in case it mattered to them. She was one of them.

"Yes, well . . ." Frank took back the conversation. "While a housewife in London, Mrs. Burke, Claire, worked for a London tabloid. Her editor asked her to do a public interest piece on the Applebee rhyme. You must remember it, Father." At the nod of his elder, Frank continued, "She spent some time here in

Applebee asking people about the rhyme with a friend of hers, a Ms. Nina Cavanaugh."

Gregory Smythe looked up at his son when he mentioned Nina's name. "Is she . . ." He began.

"She is," Frank and Walter both said at the same time.

When Nathan took note of the quick cut off of Gregory's question, Lord Gregory must have felt the need to explain and added, "Yes, I remember hearing about this Nina. I thought I was told she was here visiting someone for the summer. But I don't remember Mrs. Burke though, I'm sorry." Nathan was not sure if he believed the comment to be completely forthright, but let it pass.

"Well, we have reason to believe that Mrs. Burke may have come to harm while she was here. The kind of harm Oz would be interested in," Frank divulged finishing his thought.

Lord Gregory sat staring ahead of him for a minute or two, obviously digesting the news he had just been given. "I'm sorry to hear that." From his expression it was clear the news was more emotional for Gregory Smythe than may have been expected.

Frank continued, "I was able to look through a journal Claire had written about her time here, Father, and I actually spoke to her and Nina on their first visit. I had completely forgotten the encounter. However, she gave a detailed report of it in her journal and now, of course I remember it clearly." Nobody noticed Nathan's expression, as he bit his lip in an attempt to keep his emotions in check. This was getting all too real; bringing back history he'd rather forget. Frank continued, "It was at the tearoom, I was there for lunch and was asked to greet a couple of visitors. They asked me some questions, and we exchanged a few pleasantries. I remember them being as excited as schoolgirls. I considered them harmless."

"Harmless." Lord Smythe sat up in his seat and almost as if making an announcement he said, "We need to investigate what happened to both of these young ladies, as well as we can after so many years. I don't mean to be indelicate Mr. Burke, but is it possible our Dr. Osborne might look at your wife's body? Was there an autopsy?"

"There was. In the U.S. it is a requirement that when someone dies at home there is an investigation, and often an autopsy. In Claire's case it was required." He paused holding Lord Gregory's eye, appreciating his offer. "Since I learned of Dr. Osborne's skill, I've been wondering if he would be able to tell more from an autopsy than the regular coroners. I would very much appreciate his opinion of what actually happened to her. Thank you."

"I know this must be difficult, Mr. Burke." Frank reached over and put his hand on Nathan's shoulder in a show of support.

"I want to find out what happened to my wife, it's my primary mission, followed closely by bringing justice to anyone who harmed her. You understand?"

Frank nodded and Lord Smythe said, "Justice is acceptable; revenge is another story."

"Sometimes it is the same thing," Charlie stated assertively, and the men nodded that they understood.

Frank, hoping to cut the tension continued, "The problem at hand is we have two Americans in the village, and someone is taking an interest in them. Apparently, their hotel room has been ransacked and it's possible someone is planting listening devices in a private room. That is unacceptable. We cannot sit by and allow others' rights to be trampled. We don't want to start trouble," Frank's voice was adamant.

Charlie indicated he was correct, "And, as I understand it, it's possible the lady is becoming ill, memory loss, headaches, and some personality changes. We're concerned someone is being overzealous."

Again, Lord Smythe sat quietly before he decided what should be done. "Ashton, this is your area. Take the lead and figure out what is going on, and why . . . the why in this case is extremely important. Oh, and Ashton be careful, it sounds to me as if we have a group of malcontents." Ashton nodded his head but did not say a word.

While Nathan had been pleading his case Charlie was assessing each of the men. It was obvious that Frank was the public relations person of the group, which made sense because he had a great personality and was charismatic. Walter was older than Frank and was assisting the patriarch probably gearing up to take over when Lord Smythe was no longer up to his duties, of that Charlie felt certain. He could not decide if Walter was as amiable to outside interests as Lord Gregory appeared to be though. Ashton seemed very open and likeable, but Charlie felt there could be another personality lurking just below the surface. Easy going unless you cross him. A work hard and play hard type. Without another word, they all rose to leave. Charlie turned to Frank and asked, "So, is this the whole family?"

"Well, of course we all have our own families, wives, and children. And I have a sister, Lori. She is away at school."

"So, she is the youngest?" Charlie coaxed.

"Yes, she is the youngest. Oh, and Ashton has a couple of brothers, and of course my father was one of nine. So, technically I guess there are lots more of us out there." Frank turned and smiled devilishly. The rest of the party had walked out to the hallway, but Frank and Charlie stayed behind in private conversation.

"Do they all live in Applebee?"

"No, no, we're all over the world."

"In the United States?" Charlie's surprise showed.

"Oh sure, several in the US. Why are you so curious?"

"I find your people fascinating."

"My people?"

"Yes. What do you call yourselves?"

"Are you asking me what we call our gift?" Charlie just nodded at this question. "Are we still speaking confidentially?" When Charlie smiled and nodded, Frank said. "We call ourselves Readers."

Charlie turned and held his hand out to Frank. "Thank you for your help. If we can ever help you, just call me."

"I'll consider that a promise," Frank responded.

CHAPTER SIX

THE LIMO TOOK Charlie and Nathan back to London where they secured two rooms at the Mayfair hotel and rented a car so they could get around. Charlie texted Jo asking that they meet him at the hotel restaurant for breakfast at about 9 a.m. on Thursday.

When Charlie and Nathan came into the restaurant just after nine, Jo and Adams were already waiting. It didn't take Charlie very long to bring them up to speed on the latest news, introducing the new characters involved, namely the Smythe family. Eventually, they asked how things had been going in Applebee for the last two days.

"When we got back to our room, it had been tossed." Adams began, then waited for everyone to finish with their general comments. "We called the constable, and then had to wait because he was taking care of a cow homicide. Apparently, it's a serious crime in Applebee." Everyone chuckled. "I found a total of four bugs. I told them my wife was extremely upset and unable to sleep in that room, so they moved us to a new room. I haven't seen a bug yet in the new room, but I assume they will be busy today." Charlie held up a finger asking for a moment while he answered his phone. Nathan and the others all chatted casually while Charlie was engrossed in the phone conversation.

"That was Ashton, I told him you expected someone to try and bug your room while you are out today. Maybe a heads up will give him an opportunity to catch someone."

The waitress came over to take their orders and they all chuckled when Adams ordered a breakfast big enough for two. He commented that he wasn't eating well in Applebee, as he was concerned someone was putting something in the food. He had been trying to exist on protein bars. "How else do you explain time loss? I go down for a muffin and return 45 minutes later. I don't remember anything unusual happening, and getting a muffin from the kitchen doesn't take 45 minutes even if they have to make it from scratch! There has to be something in the food or in the coffee." Pausing a few moments as he devoured a few more bites he continued, "I figured Tuesday, we couldn't just sit in the room all day, so I planned a romantic picnic. We rented two bikes and rode around the Applebee countryside."

Jo had been sitting quietly, nibbling on her breakfast until this point. For whatever reason she decided to take over the conversation. "We rode north and found some small houses. They were sort of run down; I don't think we'd like living there. We didn't see anyone around to talk to. I guess they were all working. So, we looked around but circled back and headed south." She stopped and sipped her coffee, then continued, "There isn't anything really between the highway and Applebee except the parking area, so that was easy." Giggling and looking around to see if everyone had gotten the joke she continued, "I mean the town is really not visible from the main road at all." She explained but when nobody laughed, she continued. "Then we headed south. A little outside Applebee we ran into another group of buildings that looked like big warehouses, no vehicles, people, or anything. So, we looked around the parking area, but all we found were some boxes piled up real high. Adams thought because they were from a medical supply company it meant something, but I told him they were empty, just like the warehouses." She looked around the table at the expressions on the faces of the men surrounding her. "What's wrong?"

"Can't you hear how you sound?" Charlie asked her.

"What do you mean?" She asked as if she was going to get angry.

Adams stopped him from asking her more questions, "It's okay, Jo. Let me tell it, you eat your breakfast, okay?" She smiled at him and went back to eating her eggs. Adams' expression told Nathan and Charlie volumes, "We continued south, and came to more houses, a neighborhood. Bigger, nicer . . ." he paused and smiled at Jo, "Jo wants to buy the last house on the street because the yard is bigger." He looked over at Jo and she smiled and nodded. "We tried to speak to a few people. We'd say hello, and they would wave or maybe say hello back, smile, but nobody wanted to talk to us. If we started to approach them, they'd go inside. I actually stopped one lady and asked if she knew a place where we could stop and have our picnic. She suggested we go back to Applebee by the river. So, I asked her if there wasn't anything closer, and she said no, unless we want to eat by the side of the road under a tree."

Jo piped in, "That sounded boring." The way she drug the word out made them all laugh, and she chuckled at the fact they thought she was funny.

"We continued south and eventually came across a castle. It has a brick wall around the place, like a fortress I'd bet the wall is fortified. And they have dogs, looked like Dobies, security cameras, vehicles, all very professional." Adams finished with what he thought was a rather professional assessment of the place.

139

Charlie and Nathan were nodding their heads. "What do you think it is?"

Adams and Jo both said, "Lord Smythe's residence."

Charlie nodded "And you'd be right. We found ourselves there after our limo ride from the airport yesterday. There's a small air strip about ten minutes further south from the house."

"Air strip? You mean they don't use Heathrow?" Jo asked, truly surprised.

"Nope, they have their own. Small but efficient. As I said, it is about ten minutes south of the castle."

"How rich are these guys?" Adams queried.

Charlie chuckled and answered, "Pretty damn rich."

"I've never even heard of them before," Adams continued.

"We know. They ride under the media radar and official crap . . . or maybe I should say above it." Nathan still seemed a little in awe himself.

"Are these people, are they . . ." Adams was trying to find the right words.

"If you mean, are they Readers? They are," Charlie affirmed.

"Readers?" Adams questioned.

"Readers are what the people in Applebee call themselves."

"Okay, so you've talked to them about this."

"Just a little bit," Charlie qualified and by his tone and expression he made it clear he did not want to get any further into the details at this time.

Jo persisted, "So what is a Reader, actually?"

"Another time, Jo. All you need to know right now is they can be very dangerous if they deem you to be a threat."

Jo and Adams gave each other knowing looks. Silently agreeing that they would discuss it later, but Adams had to respond sarcastically "So, don't threaten them woman!" They all laughed, including Jo.

Jo said continuing on a more serious note, "So, what are we supposed to be doing now? Still pretending to be honeymooners?"

Charlie and Nathan sort of stared at each other. "Have you met Oscar?"

"Not exactly. I mean, I think we may have, but we weren't introduced so we don't know for sure it was him."

"You think he was the grumpy guy at the drug store?" Adams asked as if the question was only for Jo.

"Yeah, and that's when I really started to feel funny," Jo stated it as if she was just realizing this particular fact. Adams considered her assessment and thought she was more accurate than he expected. He was a little surprised that she realized it. That was when he really began to worry about her.

"I have some ideas, but I want to get with Frank before we decide on a course of action. I'll call him to see if we can get an update on Ashton's progress," Charlie explained.

They all got up to leave, and Charlie took a moment to corner Adams. "I want to speak to you privately."

Adams shook his head and walked toward the men's room. Charlie paid his bill and headed that way himself. Adams was waiting when Charlie entered the men's room.

"I think we are going to have to do some planning and investigation without Nathan's input." Adams looked questioningly and waited for Charlie to continue. "Let's say I have reason to believe Nina is involved in this more than we realized, and more than Nathan is willing to admit. He's admitted he still has some feelings for her, so I'm not comfortable depending on him when it comes to her involvement."

Adams asked if he was to keep this from Jo and Charlie quickly replied, "Oh no, I just thought it would be easier to get you into the men's room than Jo." Both men chuckled

"Did you notice how goofy she gets?" Adams asked in a whisper.

"Yeah, does she come out of it?" Charlie asked in a hurry.

"Yeah, but not all at once, it's never the same twice," Adams tried to explain briefly.

"I'll try to figure that out too." Charlie turned and as they went to leave, Nathan opened the door to enter. Charlie said, "See you out front." Adams gave a big sigh and headed toward the front door. Charlie paused to finish drying his hands and followed Adams out the door.

Adams and Jo got back in their car and headed for Applebee without waiting to say goodbye to Nathan. They were both anxious to see what condition their room would be in tonight. But then deciding not to rush they took a quick ride around the area. They wanted to focus on some back roads on the way back to Applebee. It was a relaxing trip, and the scenery was beautiful. Just when Adams thought he was hopelessly lost, he spotted a rather large building. It was old and apparently some sort of industry still in operation. Parking the car they approached what they deemed was the front door. Just as they approached the door out walked a scruffy boy of about eleven. He was wearing dirty pants, an old torn shirt, and was barefoot. He looked a little like a throwback to an old movie. "What is this place?' Adams asked.

"You aren't supposed to be here. Are you the police?"

"No, we're not the police. We're Americans," Adams responded. "We're lost."

"Oh, where do you want to go?" The boy asked proud that he might be able to help.

"What goes on here?" A sturdy man had opened the door to check on the boy's progress and was surprised to see him engaged with two visitors.

"I ran into these Americans out here, Dad. They're lost."

"Where are you trying to go? You're way off the road here."

"Yes, I've been trying to go back for half an hour," Adams offered. "What is this place?"

"Just a little side business I got, for my neighbors."

"Booze?" Jo asked.

"Yes ma'am. Would you like a spot?" The man smiled happy to offer a taste.

"Sure, come on honey, let's have a spot." Adams took Jo's arm and followed the odd little man inside. You could see the resemblance between the boy and his father. The father stood no more than 5'4" and was quite round about the middle. He seemed jovial enough, and with the little hat perched on his head he almost reminded Adams of a hobbit. Inside it was very dark, and quite damp. They could hear the gears of a water mill grating against each other, which explained the very damp atmosphere. The man pointed for them to sit at a table that looked as if it wouldn't hold the young boy. He brought out two small glasses, which might have been washed last week and then a skin full of liquor. He poured the glasses full, then set a cup down for himself and filled it as well. They took the glasses set before them and began to drink.

"Oh, my goodness," Jo exclaimed, "This is wonderful. What is it?"

"Home recipe M'lady." The man answered with a big smile obviously very proud.

Jo enjoyed being called a lady, and asked again, "Is it a wine?"

"Oh, no!" The man responded again, "Nothing so fancy for us, it's a whiskey, with a little extra touch of my own." The man refilled both of their glasses.

Grabbing her glass Jo continued to enjoy the clear amber liquid as it glided down her throat. Adams drank less than half of his and chose not to finish it. It was very strong.

"So, can we get those directions back to Applebee?"

"Applebee?" the man exclaimed, "You aren't staying at Applebee?"

"Yes, we are. We're on our honeymoon," Jo murmured.

Suddenly, the man clammed up. His expression changing it became apparent he wanted these two gone as soon as possible. He gave Adams detailed instructions and excused himself. As Adams and Jo returned to their car, Jo turned to the little boy and asked, "Why was your dad so surprised we're staying in Applebee?"

"He hates the Applebee folk. We don't talk about them."

"Why?" she sounded so innocent and naive.

"We're related to my uncle who lives there, and he and my dad had a big fight."

"What's your name?" Jo smiled again at the little boy.

"Thorny, I'm Thorny Legible," he offered with a grin that reached his eyes.

"Jo reached into her purse and took out a coin, "Well, Thorny Legible, it was very nice to meet you. Thank you very much for your hospitality," she said handing him the coin. Thorny smiled up at here just as at that moment he heard his father calling for him. His expression told Jo he didn't want to keep his father waiting, so he needed to go. Thorny ran off toward the building with just a quick wave back to the couple as they got into their car.

Adams and Jo were easily able to follow the detailed directions back to Applebee. As they rounded the first big turn to the Applebee Road, they caught a glimpse of the Applebee church. "Pull over, Adams." Jo pointed to the side of the road she wanted him to pull over onto.

"What's wrong? Did you see something?"

"I saw the church, the church in Applebee." She jumped out of the car and began to walk toward the river. Adams followed along behind confused.

"Look there." She pointed again toward the river. "It's the park, and the church."

Adams walked up behind her and stopped, hands on hips, "And this is the still we saw through the binoculars."

"Yes! That is why it looked so familiar." Jo seemed very pleased with this find.

"Yeah!" Adams tried to seem as excited as she was. "So, what does that mean?"

She stood for a moment, thinking. "Oh, not much I suppose." She sounded disappointed but didn't stop staring across the river at Applebee. "So, this isn't an island!?"

"That is odd. Did we cross a bridge?"

"Maybe. I'm not sure." They stayed awhile longer looking up and down the river, and finally decided they needed to get back. Thankfully, they weren't quite as far off track as they thought. It was all but dark when they arrived back at the inn, but they decided to take a walk through the park before retiring. As they stood in front of the church, they decided to walk around the side of the building, which included going around the big rundown house next door to the church. The property the house sat on turned out to be much larger than they thought it was. The fencing went for quite a distance to the south without ever specifically turning toward the river, however it eventually came to the riverbank. Jo wondered if the river turned, or if the land dwindled off. It was quite dark now, and Jo wanted to continue following the riverbank awhile further. The river was calm and serene tonight, and the moon shone brightly off it. They could see the funny little building on the other side of the river in the shadows. Jo was pretty sure it was the same building they spied on their first walk down the river. "Want to swim over and check it out?" Jo asked.

"No. The river is very cold, and it's probably further than you think," Adams stated rejecting her idea. Besides it's getting late.

"Come on wimp." Taking off at a dead run toward the water she began throwing off her sweater vest, and shirt. She was kicking off her shoes and unzipping her pants when Adams caught up with her and began dragging her back from the water. She fell to the ground wiggling to get away from his grasp, kicking off her pants in the bargain. Jo lept to her feet and stumbled forward splashing into the river. The four-letter epitaphs told Adams everything he needed to know about how cold it was. He stood silently on the side of the bank and helped her out of the water and into the clothes he had been gathering up as they ran.

She folded herself into his arms searching for warmth. One good thing, the brisk surprise seemed to have sobered her up. She pulled her clothes on as best she could but being wet made everything stick to her body. Then he pulled her down to sit between his legs, her back to his front. He put his arms around her trying to share his warmth with her. Within minutes she was so relaxed she was almost asleep. He was enjoying this intimate time with her and hated to disturb her. Eventually, he knew the night air was going to get almost as cold as that water, so he picked her up in his arms to carry her back to the inn. The walk was a little further than he remembered, so he sat down on a bench in front of the church with Jo in his lap. After a few minutes he moved her off his lap but kept his arm around her for warmth.

It was eventually time to get back to the room, and as he pulled her to her feet, she told him she wanted to stop by the drug store for some aspirin. She assured him that she would meet him in the room in a few minutes. Taking a firm hold of her hand Adams told her that he would go with her. Pulling out of his grasp she told him she would meet him upstairs in a couple of minutes. Since she was adamant about it, he let her go.

Back at the bed and breakfast, Adams greeted Millie who always seemed to be on duty, taking the stairs two at a time to get up to the room as quickly as he could. Entering the room he found it just as they had left it. The door string was still intact, so he began to relax. Still, he had set a few traps inside the room as well so he could tell if anyone had been inside. The dresser paper he'd left looked as if it had been left alone, and the bathroom snapper was intact, but the well-balanced coin trap he'd left on the bedside table was on the floor. "Damn," he whispered. Before going to check out the closet door trap, he looked up at the clock and saw it had been almost fifteen minutes since Jo had gone across the street. He waited impatiently another few minutes and decided it shouldn't take more than five minutes to buy some aspirin and return to the room. So, he headed over to the drug store at a full run.

Entering quietly, making sure he didn't ring the little bell set up to tell them someone had entered the store, he did not see anyone, so he walked slowly toward the back looking for any sign that Jo had been there. He continued to glance up at the mirror behind the prescription counter several times to be sure he couldn't see anyone in it. Finally he was behind the counter and pushing aside the curtain that covered the back room. Upon entering he saw the same unpleasant man sitting in a big easy chair talking to a woman who was standing in the doorway to the back alley. "What are you doing back here?" the grizzly old man yelled.

Adams noted neither of them had a weapon, so he moved into the room, "My wife came in here about fifteen minutes ago, and I'm wondering where she's gone to?"

"I haven't seen your wife," came the surly reply, "and you aren't allowed back here." Adams was certain this grumpy man had a little smile flicker across his face.

Stalling, he added, "Look we just returned from London, and we're tired. She had a bit of a headache and came over to buy some aspirin. Is there anyone else back here?"

"No, nobody is here!".

Turning as if he intended to leave, he walked back into the store letting the curtain close behind him, and quickly sent a text message to Charlie, *9–1–1, Jo's missing!* When he was sure the call had been sent, Adams rushed back into the back room and over to Oscar. "Where's my wife?" he hollered at the little man. The lady was no longer in the room, so he opened the back door and saw her just getting into a big white car. Rushing over to the driver's side door he yanked on the door handle. To his surprise it opened, "Where is my wife?" he hollered again. The lady behind the wheel smiled at him and boldly gave him the once over, although she never answered. Adams leaned into the car and took hold of her arm, pulling her from the car and back into the room.

"I haven't seen her." she said indignantly while trying to pull her arm out of Adams' grasp. He loosened his grip a little, but she stood silently looking up at him as if she was appreciating something he didn't understand.

"Oscar, introduce me to your friend," Adams attempted to put her on the defensive.

"This is my sister," Oscar stated, "and she was just leaving."

As if on cue the lady pulled away from Adams. Gathering her sweater tighter around her and adjusting her purse in her arms she said, "It's been nice to see you again, Oscar." She stepped quickly over to Oscar, who had not gotten up and gave the grumpy man a hug.

"Will I see you on Sunday then?" he asked her.

"Probably." She looked at Adams, excused herself and walked through the back door of the store. Adams went out after her and before she got in the driver's seat this time, she paused and pushed a button to open the trunk. "Want to see?" she asked knowing it was empty. Adams tapped the window of the back seat, and she turned the light on in the car that allowed him to see clearly there was no one else in the car. He moved to the back of the car just to be sure there was no Jo anywhere in the car. Coming alongside the vehicle he said, "Thanks Nina, I appreciate your cooperation." He accentuated the name Nina so she would know he knew who she was, but she just smiled at him. Without a word, she started the engine and drove off.

He didn't have time to think about this interaction, but he was beginning to panic about where Jo could be. Franticly he went up and down the alley, and then around the street looking in the windows of all the stores. He tried not to run but he was becoming more worried by the minute. Stopping several people he asked them if they had seen her, but no one had. Several of them even walked around helping him look.

On an off-chance Jo might be there, Adams decided to go back to their room. He knew he needed to contact Charlie soon, but he couldn't until he was sure she was really missing. When he noticed that, once again, the string on the knob had been dislodged, he opened the door in a near panic. Immediately he saw her laying comfortably on the bed sound asleep. "Wake up girl!" he hollered, but she did not stir. Reaching out he shook her lightly, continuing to beg her to wake up. She still did not rouse. So, he went to the bathroom and wet a washcloth and returned to wash her face with cool water. "Come on Jo, wake up." Eventually she started to stir. He heard himself give an enormous sigh and felt his chest relax just a little bit.

Jo sat up with a confused expression on her face and began to rub her eyes. "Why are you yelling at me?" Somehow she seemed vulnerable, almost childlike.

"You went to the drug store to buy aspirin one hour and twenty-six minutes ago. After twenty minutes, when you didn't return, I went to the drug store to find you. You weren't there, so I ran around this town like a crazy man looking for you. Now, I return and I find you here in the room so sound asleep that I can't wake you. What the hell happened!?"

Jo just sat there looking at him with a blank expression on her face. Eventually he continued, "Did you see the woman in the back room over at the drug store?"

"Woman? I don't remember being in the drug store tonight." She continued to yawn and then lay back down on the bed with every intention of going back to sleep.

"Hold on? Where did you go when we separated after returning to Applebee?"

"I came up here and decided to take a nap."

"No, you told me you were going to the drug store to buy some aspirin," Adams reminded her.

"I don't remember that. I just remember coming to the room to get some sleep. I'm so tired, can't we talk about this in the morning?"

"I think we need to talk about it now." He reached out and shook her again as she fell back asleep. There was no waking her this time. Picking up his phone Adams texted Charlie. *Found Jo. More weirdness. Call in the morning.*

Adams knew it was still early Friday morning when he woke up, as he could tell the sun was not completely up in the sky yet. He looked over at Jo lying beside him and wondered if she had even moved all night. Her breathing was deep and regular, so he felt certain she was probably doing all right. Quietly rising from the bed he dressed. One thing he did know is that he was very hungry, so he went downstairs to order breakfast. When he returned to the room, Jo was sitting on the side of the bed rubbing her shoulders.

"Need some help?"

"Sure, a nice rub would be great." Turning a little toward him, gave him access to rub her stiff neck muscles. Handing her a hot cup of coffee he sat down beside her and began to rub her neck as she groaned her appreciation.

He was about done with the massage, when he heard a knock on the door. "Who could that be?" Adams looked at Jo surprised. She was still not dressed, so she jumped up and ran into the bathroom.

"Good morning," Charlie, Nathan, and Ashton stood in the doorway.

"Hey, guys. What are you doing here?" Adams asked.

"We've come to check on Jo," Charlie explained. "Where is she?"

"I'm in the bathroom, why?" She was completely dressed with her hair pulled back in that extreme way she liked it.

"Because of you going missing on me last night," Adams stated plainly.

"Missing? I was here."

"Yes, after being missing for over an hour." She gave him a dirty look as if to dismiss his concern.

"Tell me what happened," Ashton asked Adams.

"We took a walk down by the river and on the way back Jo said she needed some aspirin and headed toward the drug store to buy some. I went to the room. After about fifteen minutes, when she didn't show, I went to look for her. I asked Oscar; at least I believe it was Oscar, if he'd seen her and he said no. I didn't believe him, so I followed him back into the back room, where he was entertaining a woman. I followed her to her car, and she invited me to look in the trunk and the back seat to be sure Jo wasn't in the car. She wasn't. Then I checked all over town . . . but when I got back to the room about 30 to 45 minutes later, there she is in the room sound asleep."

"See, we must have just crossed each other somehow. He wasn't here and I went to bed. I was beat."

"Do you remember coming into the room, getting ready for bed and all that?" Ashton asked.

"No, she doesn't, and she went to bed in her wet clothes," Adams pointed out.

"Wet clothes?" Charlie asked.

"I sort of fell in the river." Jo walked over and sat on the bed.

"I tried to wake her, 'but couldn't and finally she just went back to sleep. That is when I texted you."

Ashton walked to the door, "I'd like Doc to take a look at her. When you're finished getting ready, we'll be waiting downstairs. You too Adams." Ashton wanted to be sure Adams understood it included him.

After the three men left the room, Jo got up, obviously upset with Adams, and finished getting ready. When he went into the bathroom to brush his teeth, he heard her close the door behind her as she left. Rushing as best he could, he went downstairs to meet them.

"Tell me about the lady you met at the drug store?" Ashton instructed.

Adams thought briefly. "Tall, red hair, maybe 50. Sitting with Oscar Legible."

"Are you sure it was Oscar?"

"No. A crazy old man, bald, big glasses, Grumpy. Very grumpy!"

Ashton smiled at Adams but didn't respond. Instead, he led Jo outside to what could only be called a golf cart. They got in and headed toward Dr. Osborne's office. Ashton had a key card, which he swiped to get into the building. It turned out Doc's office was in one of the warehouse buildings Jo and Adams had spotted on their bike ride. It was very large, with lots of glass around the ceiling, big metal tubs, and white cabinets. It looked almost like something from a science fiction movie. As they walked to the back, Jo noticed what looked like X-ray machines, or maybe they were for MRIs. She wasn't sure. She didn't see any people. No nurses, technicians, or patients. They finally reached Doc's private office which was furnished quite comfortably. Motioning for her to have a seat in a chair in front of his desk he pulled some paperwork out of a file cabinet and asked her to fill it out.

Laying it on the desk she began with what looked like the traditional intake forms Name, address, next of kin, "Are you kidding me?" she said looking directly at him incredulously.

"Actually, I need the medical information, not so much the personal stuff."

She flipped the pages and found the list of "Have you ever hads . . ." Glancing down she said, "I've never had anything. I was shot once." And she handed the papers back to him without writing anything down.

He looked at her for a minute and decided these were special circumstances. He asked her if she wanted to put on a robe, or if she just wanted to take off anything with metal in it, including her bra. Jo had never been accused of being shy, and so she simply pulled off her shirt and bra, and then put her shirt back on. She kicked off her shoes, as she wasn't sure if they might have some metal in them somewhere. Then, he motioned for her to come into the next room with him.

"Weird!" she said a little louder than she meant to. "Now, I can see the mad scientist coming out." In front of her was what looked like a chair from a beauty shop, attached to what looked like an extra-large space helmet.

Smiling at her he proudly announced, "I had to use what I could find."

"What does this thing do?"

"It's sort of like an EEG machine. I'm going to inspect your brain. And it doesn't just show your brain waves, it's going to show any recent damage to the brain tissue or changes in pattern."

"It's going to put the picture on the big screen?"

"Yes. That's the plan." He began to expertly connect wires, and plugs, turning things on and finally returned to stand in front of her. "Are you ready?"

"Can you explain this to me. Will it hurt?" He shook his head, indicating no. Then she asked, "Why did you develop this?"

Doc pulled a stool over and sat in front of her. "We realized a long time ago, that Readers have a specific chemical in our brains that stops the brain from being burned when we are scanned. If you are not a Reader, you don't have that chemical, and when you live around Readers on a routine basis, your brain can be effectively burned— even unintentionally."

"Oh," Jo said a little surprised he even answered her question. "So, if it can happen unintentionally, can it happen intentionally?"

"That is the problem. It can, but worse than that, Readers don't have enough control to hurt you just a little bit. It's an emotional response that is not easily controlled."

"Let me understand. You're saying that if a Reader doesn't like you, or maybe he just doesn't like something you said, his ability can harm you, and you don't even know you're being harmed?" She paused a moment almost too afraid to ask the next question. "Do they know they are hurting you?"

"It's not really that simplistic, but for the most part that is correct."

"What do you mean? Is there any way to repair the damage?"

"I am developing treatments, but they have to be done very soon after the damage is caused and a very little bit at a time."

"And if you don't know you've been damaged?"

"You don't even seek help?" Surmising her next question, "It can continue to cause damage over a long period of time."

"Oh my God!" Jo responded before she realized how concerned she was getting.

"I'm sorry, Jo. But we are wasting precious time."

Jo sat back in the chair worried that his treatment was exactly what he said it was. He slid the helmet down over her head and then she felt him tightening what she was certain were screws. It appeared he was lining up her eyes with a specific spot. When he was satisfied that it was adjusted properly, he released the chair so she could lie back and be a little more comfortable.

"How long will this take?"

"About thirty minutes to get the diagrammatic pattern, and if there is any treatment needed, I'll discuss it with you when I see what it is."

At that moment the door opened, and Frank Smythe entered the room. "How's it going, Doc?"

"Just ready to start. Give me 30 minutes." Jo heard Frank make a hum noise but couldn't tell if he was okay with that or if he was disapproving.

With that Frank left. Doc must have turned on the machine, as Jo began to feel a fast vibration in the chair. Oddly, after a few minutes the vibration seemed to be lulling her to sleep. The next thing she knew, Doc was taking the helmet from her head, and returning the chair to the upright position.

Opening the door he invited the others in. Adams went directly to Jo and from the look he was giving her, he had been worried. She offered timidly, "I think I'm okay."

"Not exactly," Doc began. "I don't want to scare you, any of you," he looked at each of his visitors to include them, "but there is some damage to the prefrontal cortex. It is small, but some of it happened long enough ago that I can't get to it.

"I was able to fix whatever happened last night, at least I did my best."

"You told me you would talk to me about it before you did it."

"I did." He looked at her. "I should have told you that you might not remember it. Sorry. Side effects of playing with the brain."

"How do you feel?" Frank Smythe stepped up.

"Fine really? Any idea who did this?" Jo asked.

"No, not really," Doc answered.

"I thought it was Oscar Legible?" Adams questioned.

"The description you give of the person could be Eddy Legible. Oscar is probably 60 today. Eddy is about 79, and then of course Manny is 30, maybe, but they all look a great deal alike," Frank explained. "Have you thought that perhaps it could have been Nina?"

"Nina?" Nathan exclaimed. Charlie looked up at Frank and over to Adams. He'd hoped to avoid upsetting Nathan. "Why would you suspect Nina?"

"I assume it was Nina I met last night with the old guy at the drug store?" Adams chimed, in more of a question than an accusation.

"The description you gave does suit her. But it could have been either Eddy or Oscar with her," Frank explained.

"So why do you think she did this to me, instead of Eddy or Oscar?" Jo asked.

"Well, Eddy is too old to do much, which would be a good thing. The description could be Oscar, but does he have a reason?"

"So, we're talking about supernatural powers again huh?" Nathan let his anger show.

"Nathan, I thought you understood? We've discussed this." Charlie said trying to get Nathan to calm down.

"But why do you always go back to blaming Nina?" Nathan was so angry he got up and left. He wasn't sure where he was headed, but he needed to cool off before he said something to offend Doc and Frank. He didn't personally care if he offended Charlie at this point.

"Should we go after him?" Frank asked.

"No, he's got some stuff to deal with, just let him cool off."

"So, are you gentlemen saying you think Nina is the one who hurt Claire, and me?" Jo asked.

"Let's get Oscar and talk to him," Charlie suggested.

"We can do that . . . Doc and I can. You cannot be there. It's too likely he would strike out at you."

"Could you record the session, so we can at least hear it and eventually, if it says what I think it's going to, we can play it for Nathan? Hopefully give him some peace," Adams suggested.

"That will not give Nathan peace. Nothing would haunt him more, if it turns out to be Nina that hurt Claire." The concern on Charlie's face was palpable.

Frank nodded at Ashton, who left obviously to bring Oscar back.

Charlie looked at Jo and Adams, "You haven't read Claire's notes. In a nutshell, Nathan met Nina before he met Claire. Nina felt as if she had dibs and was upset because he chose Claire."

"That's motivation," Jo stated recognizing the implications.

"There's a book?" Frank asked.

"Not a book exactly. Claire kept notes that whole summer."

"What are you going to do with these notes?" Frank asked in a low voice.

"Are you worried?" Charlie asked with some concern.

"Wouldn't you be?" Frank retorted.

"It isn't really about you." Charlie assured him. "It's of more interest to Nathan, it's about Claire's relationship with Nina, and their visits to Applebee. I'll be honest with you; there are a few parts that could be incriminating. But I think it leads the average reader (no pun intended) to believe Claire was not quite right."

Frank nodded in understanding.

Suddenly, they heard Ashton head toward them with Oscar Legible in tow. Charlie, Jo, and Adams left through a side door, and headed back to the hotel. They made a slight side trip to the parking lot to see if the car was still there. It was gone, so they assumed Nathan had taken it. "He really must be mad," Jo announced.

"Well, I hope you two won't mind driving back to London tonight, so I can talk to him."

"Is anyone else hungry?" Adams asked. "We haven't eaten since morning."

"Do you want to eat in London?"

"How about Harrigan's?" he suggested.

They decided they would eat and then head back to London. It took them nearly 30 minutes to walk back to town. By then, it was getting dark, so they knew they wouldn't get much else done today. Satisfied, they felt like they had uncovered some interesting details that would help them solve the mystery.

CHAPTER SEVEN

THEY WENT DIRECTLY to the hotel and announced they would be leaving. Millie, who always wore her feelings on her sleeve, was the only one who seemed unhappy. She had been the only one in the bed and breakfast who was friendly with them. As she prepared their bill, she made small talk with Charlie, who they introduced as Jo's uncle. They told her that they were planning to stay with him at his townhouse for the rest of their time in England. Adams promised Millie they would consider coming back the next time they had the opportunity to visit near London.

While Adams was basically flirting with Millie, Jo was upstairs packing their things. She supposed it was the wifely thing to do, and wondered why that didn't bother her. There was a point, not too long ago, she would have complained about it just because it *was* the wifely thing to do. Once everything was packed, playing the delicate female she went downstairs and asked the two men if they would mind going up and bringing down the luggage. She was a little amazed when both Adams and Charlie seemed to puff up a little bit at being asked.

While in the room, Adams decided to check the room one last time for bugs. He motioned to Charlie by putting his index finger to his lips indicating he should stay quiet, and pointed to one, two, three listening devices hidden in the room. Amazed, Adams simply shrugged his shoulders. He would not normally tolerate a listening device to be placed in his room, and it went against his grain not to find out who kept putting them there. He would prefer to take someone to the woodshed and teach them some manners. As it stood, he would probably never know who was responsible.

Charlie and Adams carried the bags to their car parked in the parking lot and returned to finalize the bill. Jo gave Millie a big hug, which surprised her husband and Charlie both. Thankfully, Harrigan's was not very far, and it was usually a quiet place to enjoy dinner. Once their order was placed they sat staring at each other instead of chatting. It went without saying that the things they wanted to talk about should not be discussed in public, especially in Applebee. As luck would have it, their meals arrived quickly and each of them began to enjoy their food. Without conversation dinner went quickly and soon the waitress came over and asked if there was anything else they wanted. When they said they were finished, she gave them their bills and Charlie paid, as usual, with cash. Espionage 101, cash always works, and is anonymous.

As Charlie came back to the table to finish his cup of coffee, Jo and Adams saw the grumpy old man from the drug store come in for dinner with another man. The two men seated themselves without waiting to be seated. A waitress went over to them as soon as she saw them, and without reviewing a menu the men ordered.

Jo quickly wrote a note that read, "The man who just entered is Oscar Legible" and passed it around the table so each person could see it. They all took turns looking back at the two men.

Some time later, they all agreed that the older man was indeed Eddy Legible.

"I wish Nathan was here!" Charlie commented, "I don't think he's ever seen either of these guys."

"Well, if we ever see them again, at least we'll know who they are," Adams stated the obvious.

"Yeah, and run . . ." Jo quipped causing each of the men to chuckle.

No matter what they thought, relief is what they felt. Relief at getting away from these two men, who seemed to be at the base of so much suffering and unrest. Relief to be away from a strange little village where you couldn't afford to be yourself or even think your own thoughts.

The ride back to London started out in a lull. Either they had all overindulged and were ready for a good night's sleep, or more likely, they were each processing their own version of the last few week's events.

Finally, Adams broke the silence. "Do you think Nathan is okay?"

"Oh sure, he's a good guy. He just gets a little hot when it involves Claire."

"Or Nina," Adams corrected with a snort.

"So, is he still in love with Nina?" Jo asked thinking his behavior seemed more lovesick than jealous.

"Probably, a little bit. She was pretty brazen about her feelings for him. I suppose in a way it's pretty flattering," Charlie laughed.

"So, Charlie . . . did she ever go after you?" Adams asked boldly, and they each chuckled at the uncomfortable situation.

He remembered clearly the way she looked at him in the back room of the drug store. There was a moment when he felt as if she could devour him easily.

"Actually, we did almost have a moment. But we were interrupted by Nathan."

"Oh really?" Adams' tone suggested he wanted to hear all the gritty details.

"Yes, in another five minutes, Nathan would have been interrupting something very personal. As it was, as soon as she heard Nathan's voice, I was history. I don't know about you, but when you get dumped that abruptly, they don't get a second chance."

"I would question your motives if you did." Adams said trying to leave Charlie with a modicum of dignity.

Pulling into the hotel garage they spotted Charlie's rental car parked on the first floor, so they were relieved to know that Nathan was there. Parking as near to it as he could, they proceeded to the front desk to see if he had returned. He had not. While there, Charlie reserved a room for Jo and Adams. Taking the elevator up to Nathan's room they couldn't see any sign that he had been there recently. Next, they looked in the hotel restaurant for Nathan, thinking he certainly would have been hungry, but he wasn't there either. Thinking that maybe he had decided to drink his dinner, they began scouting out the local pubs. On the way back to the hotel, they decided to stop and have a couple of drinks at a little hole in the wall place next door. Two drinks led to three and soon both Charlie and Adams were feeling no pain. Jo remembered too clearly the way she felt last night and the aftereffects this morning, so she wasn't in the mood to deal with a hangover and she stopped after just one.

"You are both crazy," she said handing her tab to Charlie, "I'm going for a walk."

"Oh, come on, just relax," Adams replied trying to coax her into staying.

"I need some fresh air, and some time with my own thoughts. Enjoy!" Turning toward the door, she left them to their hangovers she knew were soon to come.

Charlie and Adams both began to enjoy the English pub, playing darts with a couple of locals, joking with the bartender, and answering questions about "the colonies", and ultimately had a good time.

Around 1 a.m., in walked Nathan. "Where the hell have you been?" Charlie asked as sternly as he could, "And don't tell me in the room . . . we looked, and you weren't there."

"Well, I've been there for the last two hours. How long have you been here?"

Adams looked at his watch, "Oh, since eleven, I think."

"Don't you think you've had enough?"

Charlie put his arm around Nathan's neck and said as seriously as his stupor would allow, "Well, what exactly is enough?"

"I'd say enough was an hour ago." Everyone at the bar laughed, "We have a plane to catch tomorrow, don't we?

"We could have." Charlie wondered, "Are we done here?"

"Sure, what else can we expect?" dissatisfaction evident in Nathan's posture.

Charlie paid the tab and the three men started back to the hotel. As they entered the lobby, Adams hesitated. He looked at his watch and told them to go ahead, he needed to check on Jo. "She's probably in the room sound asleep," Nathan suggested. He and Charlie got on the elevator as Adams stood watching them until the doors closed.

Adams figured the signal would be better outside so he walked out onto the sidewalk in front of the hotel. Flipping his phone open he hit the button to try and call Jo's cell phone.

Nothing. Hanging up, he tried once more. This time she picked up on the third ring. "Hello?"

"Where are you?" Adams queried anxiously.

"I don't know," Jo replied sounding a little upset.

"You've been walking for three hours! What do you mean you don't know!?"

"I guess I'm lost."

"Why the hell didn't you call?" Adams was definitely frustrated.

"I did . . . but nobody answered. I assumed you all still had your phones off. And I couldn't remember the name of the damn bar you were in."

Adams thought a moment and realized why he had to call twice. His phone had been off. "I'm sorry . . . where are you? Do you want me to come get you?"

"Yes, please. It's a place called Lavish. I'm on Dunden Street."

"Turn your GPS on. Do you know how?"

"Yes, I know how. Hurry." After she hung up, she fidgeted with the phone until she was sure the GPS was on.

Adams immediately went to the garage and got in the car ready to go after her. Thing twice he realized what a bad idea it was for him to go out looking for her when he didn't know London at all, and was totally drunk. He got out of the car, went to the front of the hotel and jumped in the back of the first cab he saw. "Lavish," was all he said to the driver.

Turning around, the cab driver looked at him quizzically. "You sure?"

"Yes, Lavish," he repeated. Adams fiddled with his phone until the GPS came on and showed Jo was—more than five miles away. Pulling up in front of the bar Adams handed him 30 pounds, assuming that would cover the fare, plus a handsome tip. The driver's smirk made Adams pause, wondering what he was missing.

He hadn't made plans where to meet her, so he stood in the doorway looking around, cringing at the sight before his eyes. Looking around slowly he began taking in an array of odd sights; pink and purple hair, two guys kissing in a booth, and a girl coming out of the restroom with her breast hanging out of her top. Searching the bar, he stood stone faced until his eyes finally rested on Jo, who was on stage. "On my God," he mumbled to himself, "She's going to sing!" *Should I rescue her from herself or sit back and enjoy the show.* It was really too late to intervene, so he decided it was best to just let was going to happen happen. Ordering a beer he decided to take a seat on a barstool. Noticing a few of the guys eyeing him he motioned for them to leave him alone. One small guy actually had the nerve to walk up to him and try to hit on him. Adams reached out took hold of his shoulders and turned the little guy around to face the stage, "I'm with her."

The guy was not more than a boy and said appreciatively, "Yeah, dude. She's hot."

Just then he heard singing, "You're a real tough cookie with a long history, of breaking little hearts like the one in me." His attention was drawn to the stage while he thought, 'Who knew, she's pretty good!' Getting up and taking his beer closer to the stage he stood there staring at Jo with the biggest grin on his face. *She really is hot.*

When she finished, she joined him. "That was really good," he complimented her seriously.

"I know. You didn't think I could sing, did you?"

"To be very honest, I never even thought about you singing." Taking her hand, they walked out of the bar. "You do know this is a gay bar, don't you?"

"It is?" She turned and looked back at the sign. "That explains a lot," she giggled. Then, assuming neither of them was up for a five mile walk back to the hotel, he hailed another cab.

It was after 4 a.m. by the time Jo and Adams got to sleep. They'd told the desk not to disturb them, but of course they weren't able to tell Charlie or Nathan.

As luck would have it, Charlie knocked on their door just after 7 a.m. Answering the door in a long T-shirt, Charlie couldn't tell if there was anything else under there or not, and he tried not to stare. "They've arrested Nathan!" he blurted out.

"What for?" Jo asked excitedly.

"Murder," pausing briefly, he continued, "Nina is dead." Jo and Adams both just looked at Charlie for a moment as they tried to digest this new information.

"And they think Nathan did it?" Adams finally questioned the unbelievable.

"Well, they are questioning him. I guess they can't actually accuse him until they get some hard evidence. I let him know we would come down to the police station as quickly as we can."

With that, Charlie went back to his room to make some phone calls, after they all agreed to meet at the hotel's restaurant by 10 a.m. By then Charlie hoped to have some idea of what they needed to do.

Finishing their breakfast as quickly as possible, Charlie drove them all to the police station. When they walked in, they were all surprised to see Frank and Ashton Smythe standing there waiting for them.

"What are you two doing here?" Charlie shook hands with both gentlemen glad they were there.

"We thought you might need some help when we heard Nina was dead."

"How'd you hear that?"

"Apparently, Oscar was listed as next of kin, and he figured he'd best notify us after yesterday."

"What do you mean?" Jo asked innocently.

Frank had a way of getting away without answering questions he didn't want to answer. This was one of those times. Instead, he asked Jo how she was enjoying London.

"Great. I sang at a gay bar last night," she said for effect which was not lost on either of the Smythe gentlemen.

"What did you sing?" Frank asked. Jo was surprised he would ask and laughed abruptly.

"Pat Benatar," she responded, and they both continued to laugh. Then as if choreographed they both sang out in completely different keys, "Hit Me With Your Best Shot," at the same time. Charlie was a little confused as to why they were talking about a gay bar when Nathan was in jail totally missing the tension relief that was offered.

An officer came over and handing Ashton a piece of paper, he looked it over and signed it. "What are you signing?" Charlie wanted to know.

"Release papers. I vouched for Nathan and promised to have him back tomorrow for his hearing. But they've taken his passport."

"Tomorrow? I'm impressed, that's fast."

"Well, it's just an arraignment really. Not to worry, they don't have any evidence," he said with confidence.

In less than an hour, they were walking out of the police station with Nathan in tow. "Come back and stay at our place, all of you. It's hard to know how long you'll need to be in town. You'll be more comfortable there," Frank encouraged.

Speaking for everyone Charlie replied, "That would be welcome, thank you."

With that Ashton said he needed to go by Nina's apartment and review the evidence they have so far. He'd meet them back at the house later.

It was a beautiful day and rather than sit in a room discussing what had happened with all the others, Jo decided she would spend some time at the pool alone, trying to relax. So many different conversations, plans, plots, and stories, it was all wearing on her. She had been lied to, stalked, and even had her brain examined, it was all too much. She longed for the peace and quiet waiting for her back in the good old USA.

No sooner did she wish for peace and quiet than she began to wonder where those thoughts were coming from. She was fearless, she enjoyed the fray, and nothing scared her! She thrived on excitement.

Sitting bolt upright she began rubbing her temples, 'are these my thoughts?' She wondered. *I will be glad to get out of this place.* Actually, all she wanted was to figure out what was happening to her. Suddenly, she realized she was actually having an argument with herself. Maybe she should talk to Adams about this and see what he thought. Leaning back and closing her eyes she released a stress relieving sigh.

Why was she thinking she needed to talk to anyone about her feelings? *This has to stop!* she screamed inside her head. *I just want my own thoughts back.*

As she lay in the warmth of the sun, trying to blank out her mind, she heard a commotion inside the house. She didn't get up, but she listened intently to try and hear what was being said. She heard Charlie hollering something about bullshit. He sounded very angry.

She grabbed her towel just in time to see two police officers coming toward her, followed closely by Charlie and Ashton. Her instinct told her to run, but logic told her she had done nothing wrong and, more importantly, she had nowhere to go. Chastising herself quietly, she wrapped the towel around herself feeling uncomfortable in such a tiny bikini. *I've been dressed in less at the beach with thousands of men around!* she thought. She just wanted to cry . . . *CRY? Really?*

It was too late anyway a policeman was standing directly in front of her. "Ms. Stevens. Please ma'am, we need to speak to you."

"Okay. About what?" She smoothed the towel around her making sure she was covered.

"Nina Cavanaugh." As the other young man walked closer to her, she noticed he was eyeing her up and down. It was then she decided it was too much to ask her to stand here and be questioned while they ogled her.

"If you don't mind, I would like to get dressed first, please," sounding meek even to her ears.

"Yes ma'am. Please go ahead. We will wait." The officer smiled politely knowing he had been making her uncomfortable.

Adams walked with her to the staircase and when he began to go upstairs with her, she said, "I can dress myself, you wait here." He was a little surprised but stopped dead in his tracks.

When she returned, she was wearing one of her new sundresses and had her hair pushed back away from her face with a headband. She looked like a proper young lady. "Am I under arrest, Officer?"

"Oh, no ma'am. We just need to ask you some questions."

"And I have to go down to the police station?" sounding as if she might cry.

"Yes ma'am. The detective didn't have time to come way out here."

Charlie told her they would meet her at the station, as the police put her in the back of their car. Then they stood watching the police car drive off.

As one car pulled out, Ashton pulled up in the Mercedes and hollered for them to all get in. "I haven't had this many trips to London in a very long time," he smiled ironically.

"We really appreciate your help. We'd be pretty lost without you guys." Charlie was indeed very grateful, but Nathan's nasty expression did not go unnoticed. "I'm really anxious to find out why they want to talk to Jo?"

Ashton responded, "They are questioning her because they found her Jacket in the back seat of Nina's car, and some of her skin under Nina's nails. Sounds like the two girls scuffled."

"Really?" Adams wondered. "When did she meet Nina?"

"The same day you did," Ashton spoke up. "Nina was the woman at the drug store with Oscar or Eddy, the night Jo disappeared."

Adams didn't respond but tried to pull up an image of Nina in his mind. His mind turned to that night and what he knew about it. Ashton continued, "I've also heard they don't have the coroner's report back yet either. That will shed some light on what happened when it comes in."

When they walked into the police station, they were sent straight back to see Jo. She was sitting with her legs stretched out, ankles crossed as if she didn't have a care in the world. They could have mistakenly thought she was asleep.

"You okay?" Adams asked.

"I guess so. Can I go home yet?" She replied sounding bored.

"No, I don't suppose so. Not yet." Ashton responded.

"Thanks for coming down, Ashton. I really appreciate it." Jo stood up and patting his arm looking him straight in the eyes she thanked him. It was a sincere and personal gesture and Ashton smiled at her and blushed.

Adams watched Ashton's reaction and wondered if he might have a little crush on Jo. He didn't see a wedding band, and although he may be a little young for her, it's possible he enjoyed a cougar once in a while. Ashton spoke up, "I'm sorry gentlemen, you will have to wait outside while we speak to the detectives. And Nathan, you will be next." Nathan nodded and they all disappeared into the waiting room.

Jo sat quietly while the two gentlemen exchanged information. It was finally her time to talk. "Ms. Stevens, I understand you are here as a private detective for Mr. Burke?"

"I work for Charlie Lentz, but the job is for Nathan Burke. Technically, I work for Mr. Lentz, and he took a job for Mr. Burke."

"How do you know Nina Cavanaugh?"

"I don't know Nina Cavanaugh. I've never met her."

"That cannot be correct. We found your skin under her fingernails." The police officer smirked sounding quite proud of himself for catching her in a lie.

Jo held out her arm displaying a scratch about 4 inches long on her right arm. "I was in the drug store buying some aspirin and this woman came up and started asking me some questions. She was belligerent so I started to walk away from her. She grabbed my arm, and we tussled briefly. In the process she scratched my arm. We were not introduced, so I am unable to tell you her name. I suppose it could have been Nina Cavanaugh. She seemed quite friendly with the proprietor of the store so he may know who she was, and he witnessed our exchange. He certainly can vouch for me." Jo was doing her best to keep her voice even and pleasant while answering the questions honestly without giving any extra information unrelated to the question.

"Why was your jacket found in the back of Nina's car?"

"How do you know it is my jacket?" The officer handed her the jacket inside a plastic bag.

"It was made in the Good ol' USA," he mimicked an American accent. "Is it yours?"

She took the bag and looked at the jacket carefully, "Yes, it's mine. I don't know. I don't remember having a jacket in the drug store. Maybe I dropped it when she attacked me."

"We will check on that. Can you tell us where you were between 11 p.m. and 3 a.m. on Friday night, the night of the murder?"

"I was walking lost in London."

"Lost?"

"Yes, my companions were at a bar drinking and socializing with the locals. I was bored and needed a walk. So, I took off. I got lost and called for a ride home."

"Your companions just let you walk all alone in London at night?"

"Yes, I am a grown up and capable of walking alone."

"Do you know if you were anywhere near Nina's home?"

She considered telling them about the gay bar, but wondered if it was close to Nina's house and wisely decided not to mention it. "I have no idea where Nina lives, so how would I know. And frankly, if I did know where Nina lived, as I said, I was lost so I didn't know where I was, so I still would not know." She was dead serious with her answer, but the detective asking the questions smiled at the humor of it all.

"I understand, once we have the official coroner's report, we will probably have some other questions for you, so do not leave London." He smiled trying to appear friendly.

"I'm staying at the Smythe home, and it is not in London, is that alright?"

The detective looked up at Ashton who had a big smile on his face and said it would be acceptable. He winked at Ashton.

Ashton stood and led Jo back to the hallway where the others were waiting. Next, he motioned for Nathan to join him. "The judge is in chambers so you can come back with me."

Ashton began to talk quickly, "Nathan, they already know you were at Nina's . . . fingerprints, and some other evidence." They stood, heads close together in the hallway talking frantically as Ashton tried to give Nathan some last-minute legal advice. "I can ask for a continuance if you'd like me to so we can review your testimony."

"It's not going to sound good Ashton. But I did NOT kill her. So, I'm comfortable telling them what happened." Nathan hung his head.

"I had a feeling. Okay, do it your way." Ashton let Nathan know he understood. When they entered the rather small room it looked like a real courtroom. Nathan sat with Ashton at one desk, the detectives sat at a different desk, and the judge's desk faced them and was about five feet above everyone else. Before the judge came in, the door opened and several people walked in, among them Charlie, Adams, and Jo, who took seats at the back of the room.

A bailiff stood and announced the judge and told everyone to rise. The bailiff read the charges, "Nathan Burke, you are under suspicion of the murder of one Nina Cavanaugh." He turned and addressed the Court, "evidence is incomplete at this time your honor."

The prosecutor stood. "Your Honor, currently we can prove Mr. Burke was at Ms. Cavanaugh's home the night of the murder and can prove they had a previous relationship. We have witness statements that Mr. Burke is in England searching for someone to hold responsible for his wife's death. We suspect Mr. Burke and Ms. Cavanaugh had a long-term romantic relationship starting some 20 years ago while Mr. and Mrs. Burke were still living in London. We also believe Mr. Burke and Ms.

Cavanaugh had sexual relations on the night in question. We propose, at some point in the night, they argued and Mr. Burke struck Ms. Cavanaugh killing her. We expect the motive was finding out that Ms. Cavanaugh was, in part, responsible for his wife's death."

"Review the evidence you have, Sir," the Judge directed.

"We have what we believe is sperm evidence on the sheets in Ms. Cavanaugh's bed. We are waiting for DNA matching. We have Mr. Burke's fingerprints all over Ms. Cavanaugh's home. Specifically, we have wine glasses with his fingerprints on them. We have a witness who saw Mr. Burke entering Ms. Cavanaugh's home."

"Mr. Smythe?"

Ashton stood, "Nathan is going to give his statement to the court, Your Honor. We are not presenting an actual case until we have seen the completed evidence. So, we would like to reserve the right to rebut at that time." The judge nodded and Ashton sat down.

Standing, Nathan paused in front of the table for a moment to gather his composure. He wanted to be sure they understood he was very serious about his testimony, and he needed to be credible so they would believe him. His emotions were in turmoil and although he didn't want to sound like a crybaby, but he felt that some genuine emotions during the testimony would help them believe him. He would be honest, more honest than he usually was with himself. "What the prosecutor has recounted thus far is correct. I am here because my wife died a month ago, and because the cause of death is technically unknown, we know it has something to do with some sort of brain damage, that occurred years ago. However, I do not feel it is appropriate to discuss the findings of my investigation since they are not complete," Nathan cleared his throat and continued.

"Over 20 years ago I had a one-night fling with Ms. Cavanaugh before I met my wife, who happened to be Ms. Cavanaugh's, excuse me, Nina's best friend. When I met my wife, my feelings for, and relationship with Nina ended abruptly. Nina did seem to harbor ideas that I was still interested in her, or that there was still a chance for us, but that was pure fantasy on her part. I loved my wife completely." He took out his wallet and handed the bailiff a photograph. It was a picture of Claire sitting on a tree stump in a forest. It was Nathan's favorite picture of Claire. She looked like an angel, and he couldn't imagine any man not falling immediately in love with her.

While the picture was passed between the judge, the prosecutor, Ashton, and the defense attorney, he continued, "After my wife, Claire, and I moved to the US, Claire began to show evidence of the brain damage that eventually cause her death. She suffered mentally for years; Claire is the true victim here. She was the sweetest lady and did not deserve this horrible premature death." Nathan's speech was having an effect on those listening to him. He came across as a sincerely lovesick husband. The fact that he adored his wife made his testimony irrefutable. "I have always thought Nina and Claire were best friends. Probably stupidly, I never suspected Nina of anything. During my investigation, I found reason to believe Nina knew more about her brain damage than she has ever let on. I wanted to talk to her about it, so yes; against the advice of my representative, I went to see her that night. I still did not suspect her of being culpable of Claire's injuries."

He took another deep breath, obviously trying to control his emotions. "I told her about my suspicions concerning Claire's death and she seemed sympathetic, of course. We drank a lot, and talked about Claire and the old days, we even laughed at some of our memories. At one point, maybe around midnight, I began to feel very tired, and groggy, and started wondering if she had drugged me. When Nina returned from the bathroom, she was wearing a fancy nightgown thing, and she was blonde. If you don't understand, Nina has always been a red head. I started to wonder what was going on, but I was so dizzy, I could hardly get up. She came over to me slowly and sat on my lap, kissing me on the cheek and neck over and over. She unbuttoned my shirt and pulled it off my shoulders."

At this point Nathan's voice changed, his eyes were closed, and he spoke fully from memory not assessing what he was saying at all. Many in the courtroom were uneasy as they knew he was speaking from a heart full of passion. "And oh yes, she wore Claire's perfume, it felt so good to kiss her again, I wanted her," Nathan's voice cracked, and you could have heard a pin drop in the courtroom as everyone began to understand what he was telling them. His voice told of the true emotion, and he paused for one brief moment.

When he continued, he had gathered himself, so he could continue more normally. "I heard myself call out Claire's name, as we finished. I cried, 'Claire, please don't leave me again.'" Nathan could not hold back the tears any longer, so he stopped and just stood there for several minutes.

"Then, I heard Nina scream. It was still really foggy, then she was hitting me, screaming 'wake up, wake up!' I don't know how long it took me to wake up, but when I did, I realized she wasn't in the bed anymore. I could hear her crying, 'Stop, I'm sorry.' Then, I heard a man's voice, 'You slut, we are not pigs!' And then nothing. I must have fallen back asleep, because when I woke up, I had like a buzz in my head, but it was really quiet in the house. I got up; stepping on a blonde wig on the floor by the bed. I put my pants on went to the other room looking for my shirt when I saw her." He stopped again, staring into space. "She was in the kitchen, hands tied together, hanging from the light fixture." He held his wrists together above his head, showing them how he found her. "I checked for a pulse in her ankle, but there was none. Slumping to the floor right there below her, I realized she had been killed while I was in the bedroom, asleep. So, I finished getting dressed and snuck out.

"When I got back to the hotel, I called the police and reported a fight at her home." Nathan glanced around the room, noticing some shocked expressions, and a couple of the women who had wiped tears from their eyes and smeared mascara across their faces. Then he looked up at the judge. His hand came up and wiped his mouth and it was obvious reliving the night had taken a toll on him. "I didn't kill her, Your Honor. I wouldn't kill her. I loved her." He sounded small and vulnerable, unusual for Nathan.

The judge allowed the courtroom to sit quietly for a few minutes, and then told Nathan he could sit down. The judge tried to hide any expression Nathan's story may have caused. Nathan went to sit beside Ashton and intentionally did not look back at the three friends sitting in the back row. He felt naked and raw.

"I need a couple of days to consider testimony, and I would also like to know the results of the autopsy and DNA testing as soon as it is available. Court is dismissed." The judge left quickly with the door flapping behind him.

The detective at the prosecutor's table turned and shook hands with Ashton, "Quite a tale Mr. Burke. Was it true?" Nathan didn't answer. Instead, he turned to look back at his crew. They were standing in the back looking like they weren't sure how to react. Nathan had bared his soul, something none of us ever want to have to do. How do you pretend it just didn't happen and go on?

Adams walked up to Nathan and slapped him on the upper arm. "Come on Nate, I'm buying the first round."

"Don't call me Nate." Nathan said sternly.

"No? I sort of like it. It gives you a little devil-may-care." The two men started to walk up the aisle toward the door.

"I'm 61 years old, and I have enough money to buy you, I don't need devil-may-care."

Jo followed along behind, with Charlie and Ashton bringing up the rear. Charlie heard Ashton say, "Amazing. A Brit would never live this down."

"You need to come over and hang around in America sometime. Learn not to be so serious!"

"You mean tight-assed," Ashton grinned . . . "I might just do that," he smiled.

When they arrived back at the home front, dinner was on the table. Lord Smythe was waiting in the library to speak to Ashton before they sat down and he was certain some of the others would want to clean up before dinner.

As they all began to gather at the dinner table the doorbell rang. Doctor Osborne was standing on the stoop. He had been invited to dinner; certain he would want to hear the news of the day. They were also to be graced with Marjorie Smythe's presence, Gregory's wife, and Frank's mother. She was a delicate woman of about 65. She had a beautiful smile that seemed very sincere, but something about her expression spoke of the illness Frank had hinted at. Nathan recognized it and his heart broke for the Smythe family. He imagined she was quite the woman in her younger days. He also now recognized himself in Gregory, who was obviously still completely in love with his wife and felt responsible for her condition. Nathan couldn't help but wonder if Ashton had told Gregory about his confession in court today. If he had, there was no hint of it at the table.

Frank walked in and took a seat near his mother, introducing his wife, Emily, and pulling the seat out for her, and only then, sat down beside her.

"Where are the children?" Marjorie inquired.

"The nanny has them in the tub already, mother," Emily responded.

Emily smiled at Jo, "It's so nice to meet you, Josephine. I understand you are American?"

Jo seemed to understand decorum was warranted, and instead of being her usual self, she adopted an interesting feminine guile, "Why thank you, Emily. It has been lovely visiting your country. I hope someday I can return and see more than just London."

Emily smiled back at her, sure she was as charming as she seemed, Frank on the other hand had a surprised expression on his face that almost made Jo laugh out loud. Addressing Adams, Emily continued, "I assume you are with Jo?"

"Yes, yes ma'am I am. My name is Michael."

"It is?" Frank, Ashton, and Doc all said at the same time. "Really?"

"Yes gentlemen, I have a first name. Michael Adams ma'am."

"We've been calling him Adams all day, I didn't realize his name is Michael. Do you prefer Michael?"

"Well, I used to, but I've grown quite fond of Adams." He smiled at Jo who had called him Adams since she'd met him. He couldn't help but wonder if this charming woman in front of him would revert back to the military general he'd met back in Washington.

The cook entered carrying an enormous tray of pork chops and laid the tray at the head of the table. "Maybe we can all have a prayer?" Gregory announced. "Heavenly Father, bless the food to our bodies. Thank you, Lord, for helping us sort out the issues of this day. Let each of us be blessed with Your good grace. Amen." Everyone said Amen at the same time, including Jo, who still claimed to be Agnostic.

Somehow, they knew not to discuss the problems of the day at the table. Actually, the women seemed to lead the conversation, talking about the children, and a charity event that was to be held very soon. Marjorie called for dessert to be served in the library for the men, where they would smoke pipes and cigars, and enjoy their dessert with a brandy. The ladies drew closer together and stayed at the dinner table. Jo would have enjoyed going with the men, but it was evident it was not done, so she stayed with the ladies trying to understand their ramblings. She had never thought about what rich women do all day. It was rather nice to think they sat around and tried to figure out how they could help others that weren't quite as fortunate. They had projects in the local parish and at the public schools. She would bet money they gave a big Christmas party for the orphans right here at the mansion. It was surreal, but very uplifting. Jo sat mesmerized with her own thoughts, wondering if other places in England were also caught in a time warp.

It was barely dark when Jo realized she was very tired. Looking down at her watch she saw it was after 10 p.m. She wasn't sure she would ever get used to the time difference. Excusing herself she said she needed to retire. Hearing Jo in the other room, Adams excused himself as well and they went upstairs together.

"I can't help but wonder if they haven't become quite the couple," Charlie remarked.

"It does seem so. He's quite attentive to her," Frank stated adding his own observation.

"While you older folks get ready to retire, I am going to the pub, for some entertainment," Ashton announced. "I intended to ask Jo and Michael, but it seems they have other plans."

"Just as well," Frank interjected.

In the morning Jo and Adams came down dressed for a run, both looking quite the military footmen. It had been days since they enjoyed any real exercise, and they both thrived on keeping fit. They grabbed a Danish and headed out. Frank, Charlie, and Nathan ate on the terrace as they enjoyed the gorgeous landscaping and, of course, the wonderful breakfast.

They began a discussion of recent events. Frank began by telling the two Americans what they had found out from Eddy and Oscar Legible on the day they summoned them to Doc's office. He told them Eddy admitted Nina was in the back room when Jo entered, and the two girls had a little scuffle in the store, all Nina's fault. but when Nina retreated to the backroom Jo had followed her, and Nina hit had hit her with a board and tied her hands and feet to question her. Jo was stubborn and they didn't get any answers."

Charlie broke in, "Military training 101, name, rank, and serial number."

Frank nodded in agreement, then continued, "Eventually, Eddy said he had to stop Nina, because she tended to go too far when she 'got like that' and he was afraid she would kill Jo. When they heard Adams come in, they threw a tarp over Jo, and Eddy went to move her when you followed Nina to the car, but Jo had somehow gotten loose and had taken off by then. Eddy said they had questioned her for over a half-hour."

Doc jumped in and assured them all that he had repaired what damage he had found, and he doesn't know if there will be any further damage or not.

"So, Nina physically attacked Jo in the store, then hit her and knocked her out? Is that what caused the brain damage or was there some of this hoodoo voodoo stuff during the questioning?" Charlie restated it clearly, mostly for Nathan's benefit.

Doc jumped in, "I'm sure the bonk on the head would have caused a good headache, but no permanent damage. If Nina questioned Jo, I'm sure she scanned her pretty good to get the answers she was looking for." Frank nodded his agreement.

"What kind of questions, what was she asking?" Nathan inquired.

"But you fixed the damage, so that doesn't explain the change in Jo's personality?" Charlie asked trying to understand.

"I did what I could, yes. I think I was able to get it repaired," Doc assured them.

Frank interrupted and explained that they have warned Eddy and Oscar before and both men felt certain Jo would be fine. He also mentioned they took pleasure in reminding him that his family had done worse back in the day.

"So, what is going to be done?" Charlie asked.

"We will get the council together and decide. We warned them that one of these days the entire town will pay for their lack of ethics." Frank did not wish to say anymore, so the topic was dropped.

When Jo and Adams returned from their run, the men were still sitting sipping coffee. "How far did you go?" Charlie asked as a good segway.

Adams answered, "Almost five miles, at a sprint." He paused a little bit, "She's stubborn."

"We're going to take a dip and get a shower before we eat," Jo flipped Adams with her towel.

"Did we ever have that kind of energy?" Nathan asked.

Charlie smiled, "You don't remember training treks?"

"In full gear with 50 pounds on your back. No, I don't remember that. They told me we did it, but I don't remember it." Everyone laughed.

Frank didn't mention that he himself had spent time in the Queen's Army and done two tours in Iraq. He was no slouch, but he preferred to keep his prowess to himself.

Later that day, they were all sitting by the pool when they heard someone arriving in the portico. They went out to see who it was and were treated to the most unusual sight as Lord Gregory lifted Lady Marjorie out of a horse-drawn carriage. Frank stood beside their guests and let them know, "They've been to church. And Father likes to take her to lunch at Alfredo's and if I know him, they did a turn or two around the valley. He enjoys going around greeting the "villagers" as he calls them. Mom doesn't get out much and it makes her happy to ride in the carriage." He stood smiling at his parents enjoying a moment with each other. "They may not have many chances to share these moments anymore." Pausing allowing himself to get a little emotional he continued, "Doc says my mother is getting quite bad."

Nathan didn't think about it when he said, "I recognize the symptoms. Bless her." Frank turned and walked away. He knew they lived a privileged life, but it hurt to know that you have personally helped hurt your mother. She was a sweet woman who lived her life only to make theirs better. To know your own children would never be able to know their grandmother no matter how long she lived touched him deeply.

"This is no gift," Nathan heard him say.

Two days turned into three and then four very quickly. They had been horseback riding twice once with a picnic, sailing on the river, taken a helicopter to a casino, and spent several hours in the pool. It was actually the best vacation they'd ever had. Eventually, the news came; it was time to go back to court. "Tomorrow at 11 a.m." Ashton revealed.

Breakfast was always served at 7:30 a.m. This particular morning, an extensive breakfast buffet had been laid out. Charlie, Adams, and Jo all had their luggage packed sitting at the front door ready to go. "I see you are assuming you will be free to leave after court," Frank commented.

"Well, we're hoping so. No offence, your entire family has been very gracious, but no place like home, and all that," Charlie replied.

At 10:30 a.m. they were all waiting outside the courtroom, anxious and hopeful to see the end of this situation. When the judge was ready, everyone entered the courtroom. Jo and Nathan both sat with Ashton at the defendant's desk. The bailiff announced the case one more time. This time the judge started, "Mr. Prosecutor, I understand you have an update concerning evidence?"

The prosecutor stood up and began, "Yes, your Honor, in addition to our previous admissions, we have found the cause of death to be a severely burned frontal cortex. Cause unknown." Ashton, Frank, and the others all looked at each other while the prosecutor continued, "We have a positive identification that Mr. Burke's semen has been found on the bed sheets. We have an additional witness that has identified Mr. Burke entering Ms. Cavanaugh's home with Ms. Cavanaugh at about 9 p.m. This same witness also indicates another man knocked on her door and went inside around midnight. We have been unable to identify this person but are still on the case. We have a secondary confirmation that Nina Cavanaugh did indeed scratch Ms. Abrams earlier that same evening, explaining Ms. Abrams skin under Ms. Cavanaugh's fingernails, and that Ms. Cavanaugh left the scene of her own volition afterward without seeking medical attention, therefore for our purposes unharmed."

"Is there anything else Mr. Prosecutor?"

"No, your Honor."

"Do you have a recommendation?" the judge asked.

"We have actually two separate individuals identified at the murder scene, who could reasonably have committed the murder, complicated by the fact the second suspect has yet to be identified, so has not even given testimony on his own behalf, and there is no conclusive evidence indicating any one suspect over the other. Therefore, Your Honor, we recommend that the case be determined unsolved, until such time additional evidence or suspects are brought forward."

The judge did not ask for further input, "So ruled. The parties in question are released from custody until such time there is further evidence to warrant a different action." The judge pounded the gavel, got up and left.

The prosecutor came over and shook Ashton's hand again; "I trust you will let me know when you determine anything further on this case."

"You have my word, Sir. It will be solved." Ashton shook hands briskly and turned back to join his group. They all walked out of the courtroom together outside to the curb where they saw a long limo waiting for them. "Lord Smythe has directed me to have his private plane take you back to Washington, D.C." The group stood staring at each other dumbfounded at the generous offer.

Chapter Eight

HAVING A MURDER accusation lifted from your shoulders was about as big a relief as you can imagine. Nathan was torn between following along to discuss this privately and raising a little hell. He knew there were many unanswered questions rolling around in almost everyone's head, and in most scenarios, he was the prime suspect. None of them wanted to chance some quirk of evidence landing any of them back in jail, so they all acquiesced and climbed into the limo. Charlie couldn't help but feel it was appropriate for them to return and say goodbye to the Smythe family. He felt this type of exit spoke of guilt and fear, which sat wrong with him. Had they asked him, Michael would have agreed. Jo on the other hand was still feeling the effects of Applebee, looking forward to a nice plane ride back home, without having to be squished into a coach seat.

"We'd all like to say thank you to the Smythe family, for their hospitality," Charlie said to Ashton.

"I'm sure, but they understand you have been detained longer than expected. I will express your appreciation when I see them." Ashton bowed slightly in response.

Looking at his companions Charlie gave each of them a weak smile and a nod, to which every one of them nodded in agreement. He knew none of them were anxious to jeopardize their opportunity to go home, no matter how they may have felt about the case. They had been in London almost two weeks longer than expected.

The plane was waiting for them when they pulled into the small airport. One of the benefits of having your own airstrip is you don't have to go through security or wait in lines. The cabin of the plane looked a little different than the last time Charlie and Nathan had been in it. It was set up with a few more of the big seats around the outside of the cabin and no table. It was a nice arrangement because it gave them the opportunity to visit and see each other during the flight, but they could lay back and rest if they wanted to. The flight attendant was a younger woman who spent much of her time flirting with the co-pilot. Still, she was quite friendly and made sure they each had whatever they wanted. This time they were leaving London at 4 p.m., calculating it was a 7-hour flight and a 5-hour time difference, they expected to land in Washington at about 6 p.m.

"I always conduct a close out meeting at the end of each assignment, so maybe we want to do that now while everything is fresh in our minds, and we have some time." Everyone agreed and Charlie pulled out a tape recorder so no one had to take notes. He followed a pre-designed form that he made up himself, so he would not miss anything. It took about two hours to review all the various events over the past several weeks. They decided a little break was appropriate, which amounted to a light dinner of fish and chips. When they gathered again

Charlie set out a folder he used to send paperwork to his accountant. They each went through any expenses they had incurred and signed vouchers for repayment of expenses, culminating in Charlie presenting Nathan with a bill. When he looked at it, Nathan held it for a moment as if in serious thought. He said he thought it was worth it. Then after a long pause he added almost as if he were talking to himself, "But, we didn't actually find out who was responsible for Claire's death, did we?"

He was surprised when Charlie responded, "You don't think so?"

"I thought it was clear Nina did it." Jo opined.

"As did I," Adams agreed.

Charlie stopped everyone. "Actually, I'm not one hundred percent sure we did get the answer. But I wasn't sure you wanted to continue Nathan. It has been pretty hard on you." Charlie refrained from expressing his personal opinion and stated what he knew Nathan felt. "If memory serves me, Doctor Osborne wanted to perform an autopsy on Claire's body. Shall I assume you will be alright with doing that?"

Nathan thought about it a long moment. "So, you both think it was Nina?" The disappointment sounded in Nathan's voice. Then he continued, "I think the autopsy is a good idea, but I'd like to stipulate he do it at home, not in England."

"Well, I'm sure he can do it in Washington, when he returns." Nathan nodded his agreement and Charlie added, "I'll have papers for you to sign before you go back to Maryland." Charlie was encouraged that Nathan was still interested in completing the case. "Nathan, could I please borrow Claire's manuscript so I can complete my assessment of it? I would like to have a complete translation of it. We didn't quite finish."

Nathan was looking at Charlie with a confused expression.

"I thought you, had it?" He pulled open his briefcase and rummaged through it with no luck. Charlie grabbed his brief-case and did the same thing. "Where was the last place we had it?" Nathan asked.

"Did we take it with us?" Charlie thought back.

"Yes, I'm sure we did. Remember we discussed it with Frank, and he asked if he could see it. Did we show it to him?" Nathan reminded him.

"He asked if he could borrow it," Charlie corrected Nathan's memory.

"And we side-stepped the request." Both men stared at each other. "That was the day Dr. Oz did the brain scan on Jo, wasn't it?" Nathan remembered.

"I believe that is correct. Did we have it with us at Oz's office?"

"I don't remember." They all agreed they didn't really remember.

"You know fellas, I don't feel so bad not being able to remember some things. It seems I'm not the only one who is having that particular problem," Jo joked, but with serious undertones. All the furrowed brows told of their agreement with her statement.

Nathan was the most disgusted with the possibility of having lost the manuscript as he too wanted a full accounting of what Claire was trying to tell him. "You know, I feel that Claire really wrote the manuscript for me. The article she wrote didn't follow it at all, so she didn't write it as notes to write from. I think she knew she wasn't going to be able to tell me everything, so she wrote it down.

"And it was all wrapped up tightly, with a bow, just like a gift," Jo chimed in.

Deep in thought about Nathan's sentiments Charlie offered, "You could be right, Nathan. Maybe they are her last words to you." Charlie realized as soon as the words left his mouth this fact would inspire Nathan to continue in his search. This case was not over.

"So, did you ever hear the tape they made of the interview with Oscar Legible at Doc's office?" Adams asked.

"No, Frank and Ashton both mentioned it and told us pieces of what he said, but they never played it for us," Charlie stated with some sarcasm in his voice. "Did you ever feel they 'niced' us into forgetting what we were about." When everyone looked at him blankly, he explained, "They were so nice, we forgot they weren't really on our side."

"So, we took our eye off the ball . . . we were so happy to get out of there, we didn't finish the job," Adams said with realization in his voice.

"Well, they weren't against us!" Nathan assured them of his opinion. "I could still be sitting in an English jail if it weren't for them."

"Me too," Jo agreed.

"Is it possible they played their little mind game on all of us. It just affected us differently," Adams suggested. They each thought about Adams' words realizing the full implication of the possibility. You couldn't actually trust them about anything, because if they could make you believe something, even if it was only to cause you to forget it, you aren't able to accomplish your goal, even when you think you did.

"Fine, I'll give Frank a call and tell him we want the manuscript back and that we'd like a copy of the tape." Charlie offered, "Let's start by assuming it was just a forgetful moment with too much going on. We need to make sure we remember they are not the enemy, but we do not have the same goals either," Charlie whispered looking over his shoulder for the location of the flight attendant.

"And we need to learn something from Claire," Nathan also spoke in a hushed voice, "Write shit down. You may forget, but the notes will remind you. At this suggestion they all nodded their heads.

Unanimously agreeing they were all a little tired, they decided to lay back and relax before landing. After all, apparently the case was not over.

About the Author

DS LARANCE GREW up in New York and moved to Florida at a young age, embracing the change despite being away from her family. She dedicated 36 years to government service, earning respect for her commitment. DS and her husband have a supportive family with one son and a granddaughter. Now retired in Clearwater, Florida, DS enjoys writing and has published her first fictional book, embracing new adventures and passions in her retirement.

If you enjoyed this book, please follow the author, and join the Facebook Group https://www.facebook.com/groups/ debsuestories